Advance Praise:

The Town Where All Things Are Possible made me want to pack my bags. The pages are filled with mystery, loss, and love all wrapped up in one weird, little town full of strangers I have always known.
This book, this town, is exactly what we need right now, a delightful mystery filled with hope and, of course, possibility.

—Karen Feiner, *The Shakespearean Shrew* Podcast

Beautifully written fable of love, community, and what dreams might cost. This book is full of humor, warmth, and life and it's populated with a rich collection of characters (and penguins!) that you will quickly grow to love and want to spend more time with.

—J Hall, *The Okie Bookcast*

In The Town Where All Things Are Possible *introduces a cast that feels both deeply whimsical and deeply human. There is so much thought and empathy poured into this story that, as a reader, I found myself falling in love with The Town just as much as Alexandria does. Just like her I wanted to get to know everyone and explore all of the mysteries of how the community functions.*

—Grimsley Sloane Arvizo, *The Writer's Co-Op*

IN THE TOWN WHERE ALL THINGS ARE POSSIBLE

By Charles J. Martin & Will Weinke

LP
LITERATI PRESS
BOOKSHOP & COMMUNITY

Cover Image By Nick Geist and Charles J. Martin
Edited by Rebecca Rutledge
In The Town Where All Things Are Possible Copyright ©
2014 by Charles J. Martin.

For my beloved bookstore, our staff, the storytellers, the artists, the editors, the readers, and all the others who've made our magical ideas possible.

Contents

A simple job

In The Town Where All Things Are Possible,

there lived a simple man with a simple job that, improbably, held a magical world together.

The town nestled itself between twin mountains with their backs to the ocean. At the town's edge, a cliff dropped a hundred feet to waves crashing into a sheer rockface. The mountains protected the town with a brotherly affection, only allowing the gentlest of weather to pass between their sturdy shoulders.

Tourists and travelers agreed that the residents were singular in an odd yet fetching way. They smiled without cares, they walked everywhere that was worth traveling to, and they had become so accustomed to the uncanny that they breezed through life with the absolute belief that everything would work out in the end.

And it did, for the most part. Yet just as storms slipped past the mountains from time to time, so did troubles.

This is why, tourist guides proclaimed, every citizen of The Town Where All Things Are Possible sang so beautifully. It was how they healed; it was how they understood. Every third Thursday at noon, the town erupted in song. Every able hand played guitars, hand drums, clarinets, washboards, and all other manner of noisemakers for one hour of songs. Sometimes they played as one, other times the town was a chaos of sound and sentiment.

Music filled the other days too, with an optometrist often sitting on his balcony at lunch playing his trumpet to a toothy seamstress across the alley cradling a violin in the crook of her neck. The plumber hefted up her burping tuba for a mid-afternoon pick-me-up, the funeral director sat at his pinging harpsichord over coffee, the landscaper snapped on his vest full of breathy harmonicas the moment his day's work was done. Most citizens played soft and humble, but those who performed loud and daring were encouraged to perform loud and daring at a time and place deemed appropriate by their neighbors.

And the same was true for so many other things: painters and magicians and athletes and dancers. Poets and actors and bakers. Even politicians found their chosen talents welcomed within reason. One could be good at anything and be happy, but when one chose to be great, that is when suffering followed.

Yes, even sadness was possible in this magical town. When death arrived to claim one of its citizens, the town closed its roads for a funeral march. The town's celebrated pink roses would appear on every stoop. The school liberated its students, shopowners shuttered their windows and locked their doors. All would join the march and help shoulder the sorrow as one.

Those who chose to be great were the ones who fled, seeking out grander communities around the world. Though all things were indeed possible, the town itself could not grow large enough to attract multi-billion dollar corporations or financing titans, nor could it produce the materials to construct towering sculptures or field the vast armies needed to engage in heroic wars—the kind that made men into legends.

In The Town Where All Things Are Possible, the townspeople embraced each other's quirks, but all detested selfishness. That is why the great men and women left, for greatness sprouts from selfishness.

"Perhaps we should just rename it 'The Town Where All Small Things Are Possible'," the mayor suggested regretfully after her child announced their intentions to chase stardom overseas. Her husband insisted the town's name was already long and clunky, so the mayor dropped the idea and turned her focus to the things she could change.

The smaller things.

And so the town endured, the waves grasping up the stone face of the cliffs, the winters and summers shuffling in and out without a fuss, the townspeople achieving admirability in their own unique ways, and the small stream of tourists making the long trip to see if the town lived up to its name.

All the while, The Man Who Held The Town Together toiled, spurning vacations and holidays. He believed his job was too important to abandon, even during the Thursday noontime musical jamboree. Since accepting his position at the age of eighteen, he'd only taken two leaves of absence:

1. A stomach flu put The Man down for a weekend, which resulted in:

    a. The librarian finding her husband in bed with his nineteen-year-old viola student on Day One

    b. A family of five dying in a house fire on Day Two

2. The Man slept in on the morning after his wedding, which resulted in:

> a. His bride slipping away to the store for a dozen eggs,
> b. His bride dying alone on a cobblestone street while the killer escaped without a trace

He then vowed to do his work every day in his tiny office on the hill—no matter the cost. Until he drew his last breath, he would accomplish this small, yet critical task to protect the town from the darker end of possible.

This job was done mostly in secret. It was done entirely alone. The townspeople didn't understand what he did in his tiny office day after day, but they knew it was important. There had always been a Man Who Held The Town Together and likely always would be until the town fell into the ocean.

They also knew The Man grieved. Though they worried for him, they left him to create a life that could sustain him. How he dealt with his loss was no one's business but his own.

The Man was not a hermit, though. He forced himself out into the world out of a sense of duty to the town he adored. The Man fashioned himself into an excellent dart thrower, though he secretly believed it to be a silly pastime. He also attempted writing, but so much bitterness boiled within his heart that he feared anything he scratched out would only hurt and worry those around him, so he abandoned the pursuit and doubled his efforts on the tavern's well-worn dartboard.

He was town champion four years in a row.

The Man remained alone.

"Love is a perfect and necessary thing in the Town Where All Things Are Possible," the Man's father implored after insisting himself into his son's small office one day. This was during the one day a week when his father's memory returned, a time more precious than the sun for the Man Who Held The Town Together.

That day, his father brought chicken salad and declared The Man would learn to like it, finally after all these years. His father also insisted it was time for The Man to try out love again, finally after all these years.

"You see," the father said. "Love is the only great thing we have, because no matter how grand it may be, it is still confined within the hearts of only two people. You must find love, my boy; that is your duty to me!"

But the Man Who Held The Town Together did not believe it, knowing love was too big a thing for what was left of his ravaged heart. He no longer possessed the fire for love. Or what little fire he had left only kindled for a woman no longer in this world.

The Man remained alone.

One spring day, a wind whispered its way through the valley and into the town, bringing with it a tired commuter bus. Inside were:

Tourists hoping to find a charming postcard to add to their collection and to gather a bouquet of pink roses

An elderly couple returning from a long, trying vacation visiting their feral grandchildren

A traveling salesman wondering why he still bothered

making the long trip to a town whose people had shown so little interest in the latest advances in vacuum cleaner technology

Also, in the very back of the bus, keeping to herself, was the new owner of The Wider World Books and Novelties.

Her name was Alexandra and she'd never even heard of the Town Where All Things Are Possible until her distant aunt's last will and testament named Alexandra the bookstore's successor. Up until the moment she received the certified letter, Alexandra had lived a slow, safe existence with a slow, safe partner who hosted slow, safe dinner parties for friends who rarely seemed her own.

She still remembered being a bold child so certain that she'd grow to be a bold adult just like the aunt who'd left her this strange inheritance. She remembered sitting in a creaking pine tree as a child, searching the horizon for a fantastical place just like The Town Where All Things Are Possible. She knew it must exist somewhere and one day fate would lead her there.

And so it did.

In The Town Where All Things Are Possible,

there existed a subtle slant to the land. It sloped on all sides to form a funnel directing the town's excess rainwater toward a single sewer drain grate in the town square, hardly changed since it was first built 150 years prior.

Children made a game of watching multicolored marbles chart out an odyssey from the cliff's edge, through the streets and walkways, across the market, bounding down stone steps and cobblestone streets, and finally clinking through the ancient, cast iron grate. The vibrant marbles clattering down the stone walls of the sewer sent up musical echoes as they plummeted into what the children's grandparents claimed was the center of the world.

"But now we just call it God's Blowhole," Wendy Fastly, the town librarian, told Alexandra as they both watched boys lying beside the storm sewer, waiting for the next herd of marbles to navigate the town streets and plummet through the grate. In Wendy's lap was a wide ring of keys of all kinds. Next to Wendy sat a thin, kindly old man with lovely silver hair and a welcoming smile. It was not the day of the week when he remembered, so instead he greeted all who looked his way as if they'd been the longest friends.

"So nice to see you again," the old man said, taking Alexandra's hand in hers.

"Um, yes," Alexandra said, glancing at Wendy who nodded for Alexandra to play along. "Can you remind me of your name?"

"Oh, it's fine, I forget everyone these days," the old man said. "Just Jonathan is fine. My boy is the one who works on top of the hill. He holds the town together, you know. He's a mess."

"I see," Alexandra said, then tucked her long, gently-curled red hair behind her ears. She glanced from the old man to a mischief of boys approaching from the outer edges of the town square just as marbles clattered and bounced ahead.

The boys raced to surround the grate, then watched the colorful racers plunge, pinging against the walls on the way down to who-knows-where. Alexandra waited to hear the marbles hit bottom. They never did.

Then a horrid clanking startled Alexandra. The boys, the librarian, the kindly old man, and Alexandra all turned as a metal cart clattering down stone steps toward the town's center. The Man Who Held The Town Together scrambled after, his knobby knees pumping, his hands grasping for the handles just out of reach.

Upon reaching the last step, the cart tumbled forward, and boxes fell and gasped out hundreds of yellow notecards.

The children giggled while Alexandra abandoned her luggage and helped The Man Who Held The Town Together collect the debris spread out across the town square. The Man darted this way and that with a manic fear of losing even a single notecard to the wind.

"There's my boy!" the kindly old man said. The boys and the librarian all laughed at the spectacle, but Alexandra felt sorry for the fellow. And a little curious too.

Upon stuffing what he thought was the last card into the box, The Man tipped the cart right side up and reloaded its burden. He apologized profusely as his gaunt yet handsome face brightened to a warm red. Alexandra presented one last notecard, which The Man snatched swiftly.

"I'm sorry, just, I need these," The Man stammered, but when his blue eyes rose to take her in, they both fell silent for so long that the boys and the librarian all looked away, uncomfortable. The kindly old man gleamed a hopeful smile.

Then the old man's smile faded into a curious expression. "Who is she?" he asked, pointing to Alexandra.

"Alexandra. She'll be taking over the bookshop."

He nodded, then looked at The Man. "And who is he?"

"Your son," the librarian whispered.

"Oh, right. He holds the town together. He's a mess."

The librarian patted the hand of the old man and whispered, "Be nice, Jonathan."

Alexandra pretended not to hear, instead focusing on the strange, charming man and his cart of precious notecards.

"Must be critical intel from a war long ago," Alexandra said, eyebrow raised in a daring and lovely way. "Or perhaps torrid love letters from your grandmother's grandmother."

"Ha, yes, that would be something," The Man said, finally looking from her face down to the cobblestones between them. "No, not quite so interesting."

The Man attempted to comb his mussed, black hair with his fingers, but it fell back into its usual disarray.

"Wendy, father, boys; how are you today?" The Man called to the witnesses.

"We're fine, just enjoying the sun," Wendy said, patting his father's hand. The old man had lost his grasp of the conversation and was watching the clouds pass.

The Man turned to take in the state of his cart—intact and functional aside from one slightly bent wheel. Wendy sent Alexandra a knowing wink which told Alexandra everything she needed to know about The Man Who Held The Town Together.

He stuffed the note into a box, then pushed the cart around to begin the laborious task of lifting it up the stone steps, one heavy clank at a time.

Alexandra looked from The Man to her bags, then back to The Man. She took a hesitant step toward him.

"Go," Wendy whispered with a smile. "We will see to your things."

Alexandra hesitated, watching The Man Who Held The Town Together struggle.

"He is in need of your help more than any man you will ever know," Wendy told Alexandra. "But he's worth the trouble."

A watchful town

In The Town Where All Things Are Possible,

there existed a small, one-room office lit by a lone bulb which couldn't be turned off. This humble building, not quite a shack but near enough, was perched on top of the town's tallest hill. A steep walk up five blocks of cobblestone led the way for anyone who wished to visit. The door did not lock; thieves in the town were rare. Even if a burglar did happen upon the office, they would find nothing of value to anyone but the office's lonely resident.

So the town's curious neighbors were surprised to witness two people making that morning climb instead of one. Window shutters creaked open and gossip-hungry heads popped out to watch the widower and a red-headed stranger force a heavy cart up the difficult path.

Squeak, clank, squeak, clank, squeak, clank, protested the cart as it hobbled up the hill, The Man pushing from the back, Alexandra pulling from the front.

"Do you do this every day?" Alexandra asked, drops of sweat beginning to soak into the collar of her blouse.

"No, just once a quarter when things need sorting," The Man Who Held The Town Together replied.

"What exactly is it that you do?" Alexandra turned her head to check their progress. Two blocks to go.

The Man wanted to reply, "I hold the town together," but was afraid she wouldn't understand. Instead he answered, "I keep bad things from happening to good people."

He realized too late that his second answer was no better than the first, but Alexandra rewarded The Man with an amused smile.

"So wartime secrets it is!" she quipped. "Who are these scoundrels banging at our gates?"

The Man blushed.

"Hold on!" a voice called, and they turned to see Mrs. Milda Gratherson clicking her walker speedily up the hill. "I need to talk to you!"

The Man Who Held The Town Together paused and looked down the hill towards the frail woman braving the steep climb.

"It's okay, Mrs. Gratherson!" The Man called. "We are almost there, we don't need your help."

Alexandra motioned to the woman. "Should we perhaps go to her?"

The Man smiled and shook his head. "She'd be offended." He took a quick moment to admire Alexandra's glow as she fanned herself, eyes coyly looking away. He remembered the game; he remembered his wife had once played it.

A tumble of emotions followed and his face tightened for a long, heavy moment. Long enough for Alexandra to notice.

"Are you . . ." she began.

"I only need a moment of your time," Mrs Gratherson called, still struggling with the hill.

"Are you sure we shouldn't?" Alexandra asked. Again, The Man shook his head.

The Man leaned over the cart, gesturing Alexandra closer so he could explain in confidence that the town was once a hotspot of political activists. Mrs. Gratherson was one of the few suffragists still alive and made it widely known that she didn't live this long by taking the easy way out.

"Ah," Alexandra replied, as if that explained it all. She paused to do the math in her head. "You can't mean women's suffrage. How old is she?"

"I don't know and I wouldn't recommend asking," The Man said, smirking. They waited for Mrs. Gratherson to click her walker closer. The twin mountains allowed another gentle breeze to pass through to cool the laborers.

"It is such a beautiful day." Alexandra sighed as she turned her face to the sun, absorbing its life.

"Hold on, almost there!" Mrs Gratherson called, taking a moment to wave, ensuring she'd been seen.

"Take your time," Alexandra said, then turned to the Man. "So, Mr. . . ." Alexandra waited for him to fill in the blank. His face darkened ever so slightly and his eyes dropped away. "So," Alexandra said, taking another tack. "Are all things really possible in The Town Where All Things Are Possible?"

The Man brightened, a coy smile forming. "Within reason. We answer the question quite a lot, as you'd imagine."

"Surely. I'd found nothing definitive in my exhaustive research before coming and the tourists on the bus were no help. Most assumed you'd just come up with a clever name to draw them in."

"Well, the town's not quite as magical as you'd hope," The Man said, though he knew better than anyone that the town was even more magical than people hoped.

"Oh, that's very disappointing," Alexandra said.

"It is, but also it isn't," The Man said, which answered

nothing, as he had intended. "There are things that are too big for such a small town, but if you can fit your dream within our humble borders and those dreams don't interfere with the dreams of others, then yes, your dream is most certainly possible."

"How curious." Alexandra nodded her head as she thought. "So, I can think of any ridiculous, yet unobtrusive request, then it just appears in front of me? Like a fried cherry pie will just *POOF* right here in my hand?"

"Not exactly *poof*. But if you put a little effort into it, somehow it will come true."

"Ah." Alexandra nodded again, assessing. "Right, I would like to ice skate this evening to celebrate my entry into the marvelous Town Where All Things That Can Fit Within The Town Where All Things Are Possible Are Possible! Make it happen."

The man chuckled and turned back to Mrs. Gratherson, now only a few feet away, clacking her walker to gain their attention.

"Mrs. Gratherson, what emergency can we thank for your presence?" The Man asked the winded old suffragist.

"Hardly an emergency, but a thing that simply could not wait!" Mrs. Gratherson leaned against her walker, then pulled out a handkerchief from her sleeve with a magician's gusto. She dabbed off the sweat from her brow.

"Come close to me, boy. It's a secret," Mrs. Gratherson said.

The Man glanced back at Alexandra, who nodded for him to attend to Mrs. Gatherson. The Man closed the last few steps to the old woman, then leaned in to retrieve the secret.

"She is quite pretty, this one!" Mrs. Gratherson exclaimed rather loudly, then squealed out girlish laughter. The old suffragist turned and clicked her way back down the hill. "Don't screw it up!" she called over her shoulder.

The Man took a few moments for the embarrassment to properly set in, shoved his hands in his pockets, then swiveled slowly around. Alexandra was laughing into her hands, but managed to steel herself and grasped onto the cart, ready to resume.

She looked up at The Man, eyes narrowed. "Shall we?"

"Yes, of course."

"Oh, one more thing!" the old woman exclaimed over her shoulder.

"Yes, Mrs. Gratherson?" The Man called back.

"I have some fried cherry pies for you," Mrs. Gratherson said. "I'll have my boy deliver them both to you this evening!"

The Man met Alexandra's stunned eyes.

"Poof," he said while flaring out his fingers like an explosion. He turned to wave at the old woman. "Yes, thank you, Mrs. Gratherson! And can you have your son check on the ice rink, see if maybe we could get something ready for an evening celebration of our town's newest resident?"

Mrs. Gratherson clapped and squealed.

"Lovely idea, my boy! I'll have him do it right away!"

The Man turned back to the cart and Alexandra's mouth hung open.

"How is that even possible?" Alexandra asked. "It's not even fall yet."

"Oh, haven't you heard? This is The Town—"

Alexandra groaned. "Yeah, yeah, I know."
Squeak, clank cried the weary cart.

In The Town Where All Things Are Possible,

there was once a boy named Wallace who wandered the streets with a cheery, freckled face and hair that sprouted like weeds in an abandoned flower garden. He rarely talked to anyone but his three trusted friends: Leo, who would inherit the town's small golf course; Wendy, who would inherit her mother's role as librarian; and the boy who would soon become The Man Who Held The Town Together. As far as the townspeople knew, Wallace was without a home and without a family, but he seemed well fed and never caused a commotion, so was left to find his own sort of happiness.

"Is Wallace still around?" Alexandra asked while gazing at a small black-and-white photo of the boy hanging from The Man's wall above a tidy desk. A tall, strange contraption sat in the middle of the office, nearly reaching Alexandra's eyebrows as it clicked and hummed with tiny gears, gleaming brass, and a stack of blank notecards on top. The Man Who Held The Town Together took a moment from moving boxes from the rickety cart into the corner of his office to look over Alexandra's shoulder. An ancient incandescent lightbulb shone above them.

In the photo, the boy smiled with all his teeth, which leaned and slouched inside his mouth like a crowd of jaded teenagers. His jeans were ripped at the knees, his shirt splattered with assorted stains. He looked rambunctious, poorly supervised, and happy.

"He hasn't been seen in years," The Man replied as evenly as he could. He returned to the boxes. "We were the same age. Are the same age."

"Was he a—," Alexandra started, but stopped herself. "Is he a relative?" She turned from the photo.

"No," The Man said. "But he was as close. When I took this job, I hung the photo up as a reminder."

"A reminder of what?" Alexandra asked.

The Man wanted to answer, *To keep working, always,* but instead answered, "Of why I do what I do."

Alexandra was not certain how to react, so instead opted to change the subject in the gentle way her mother taught her for when moments became too complicated and heavy.

"Tell me more about your job," Alexandra asked, plopping the last box down on the pile and wiping dust from her hands.

The Man took a moment to formulate an answer. "Not much to say, really. Just sorting information." He gestured to the strange ticking contraption on his desk. "Messages come in, I put them in the right place, then retrieve them later if needed."

Alexandra took a closer look at the contraption, its wires and spinning ball bearings all alive and moving in time. Little rollers pressed down on the top notecard, then slid it down a ramp to disappear into a little box. Something whirred within, coming to life as other gears spun and ticked. Slowly, the card began inching out of the bottom of the box.

"Pardon me," The Man said as he stepped to the machine, blocking her view. Alexandra retreated to give the Man room to work. She saw a flash of black text that was remarkably similar to handwriting as The Man swept the message out of the contraption. He glanced at the text while keeping the card faced away from Alexandra.

"Is it secret reconnaissance from some exotic war?" Alexandra asked.

The Man laughed. "No." He stepped around her, careful not to let her see what was written on the card. "You know that person whose job is so boring and technical that it's impossible to remember what they told you they do each day?"

He moved one box to get to the box underneath, then flipped open the lid.

"That's me. That's my job."

He thumbed through the cards until he found the right spot, then slid the card in. He closed the box, then faced Alexandra. "I do it because no one else has the patience."

"Ah." Alexandra's attention turned back to the strange machine. It wasn't plugged into the wall. A thin antenna sprouted from the top, trembling at the moving clockwork.

"Are you good with machines, by any chance?" The Man asked.

"No, not at all," Alexandra said.

"Ah, too bad. Our town is in need of a tinkerer for when the machine breaks down."

"Shouldn't the spy agency who supplied it to you have someone on staff to keep your enigma machine running?"

"Again, it's not that interesting," The Man said. "But there is some secrecy involved. Like a lawyer working in a very boring section of real estate law."

"And what happens if the machine breaks and there is no tinkerer around to fix it?"

"There will always be a tinkerer," the Man said. "The town will provide."

Alexandra took in The Man fully as he turned to fuss with the small half-pyramid of boxes. He was handsome in a quiet, scholarly way, but overworked and sad. She'd always promised herself to never date a man as addicted to work as her father, but she failed time and again. Looking over The Man, she knew they would date; she felt her heart tugged toward him as if the planet's entire gravity had shifted the moment they met.

The tinge of fear was comforting. Before meeting the pediatrician, she fretted that she'd become too old to wave her love fearlessly as she had as a child. So she started dating serious, steady men because she'd come to believe that love was a somber business, a measured gamble. Love meant loss, either through death or abandonment. She'd lost loved ones in both ways by crushing amounts.

The mature thing to do then was approach love as a risk to be mitigated. And so she dated men like the pediatrician. He was kind, he was generous, he was safe. There was no mystery to the pediatrician. It did not take a daring heart to love men like him.

But this one, The Man with the intriguing job and an endless supply of cryptic replies, he was one who would take a daring heart.

It was thrilling. She would see it through, she must.

"Well, I have my work and you have your unpacking," The Man announced, finally turning to her and offering a handshake.

The abrupt banishment from the office coupled with

his kind smile had her wrong-footed. Within the time she hesitated and her heart fumbled, she pictured their lives together. A mysterious bookshop, his mysterious work, and between long ocean voyages to distant lands, they would wake in the charming town and take walks to the town square for quiet mornings of coffee, gossip, and rustling newspapers.

Does The Town Where All Things Are Possible have a newspaper? If so, what would it be called?

Then she realized she'd been quiet too long. Her head wrestled her heart back into its chest, but not too deep. "Yes, right. My good deed for the day is done."

She backed out of the small office, tripping on a cobblestone and flailing briefly to regain her balance.

"Mind your step," The Man said, reaching to offer his hand. But she was sure-footed again and in no need of help. His hand lingered between them like a chess piece to be considered. She didn't trust herself to touch the Man's hand, not yet.

"Thank you," she said, with a nod of the head. She turned and retreated back down the hill, aglow. Her heart felt nimble. She could still be fearless. Her sister would be so proud.

A rookery

In The Town Where All Things Are Possible,

there lived a small family of rockhopper penguins that simply refused to live amid their brethren. How they found themselves in The Town Where All Things Are Possible, half a world away from normal migration patterns, is unknown. Most assume it had something to do with a child's daydream.

Regardless, the five flightless birds with flourishes of yellow and black feathers sprouting from their brows quickly endeared themselves to the townspeople. The penguins strutted amongst the community like a displaced English New Wave band. They could be found every morning on the southern tip of downtown, padding their way toward a thin trail winding to the waves far below, then returning in the evening with bellies full of fish. The chatty family exchanged squawks and casual nods with their neighbors, spent quality time in the town square while visiting the town grocer, and could be counted on to appear at most holiday events. Then they'd retreat to the toolshedLeroy McMurry had gladly abdicated once he'd learned the penguins needed a home.

The plucky welcome committee of rockhopper penguins met Alexandra as she wandered the narrow and winding streets in search of her new store, The Wider World Books and Novelties. A mist had settled on the town after sunset, so Alexandra couldn't make sense of the silhouetted group padding their way towards her. Then she gasped and the penguins fluttered and hopped. The eldest penguin boldly stepped forward and squawked. He was nicknamed "Billy" for his un-penguin-like blonde, spiked feathers that resembled a pop singer's hairstyle of the same name.

Billy stopped a few feet away and the other penguins bumped against one another, like a train rumbling to an abrupt stop. Billy took a few moments to assess the newest citizen of The Town Where All Things Are Possible, then squawked loudly with a flap of his wings.

"Oh, is that so?" Alexandra asked, crouching down to their eye level. "My name is Alexandra and I'm looking for The Wider World. It's a bookstore of some sort."

Billy warbled, then pointed his beak toward the left-turn of an impending fork in the road. He shook his feathers, squawked again, then resumed leading the procession's long journey home. The smallest penguin and last in line kept an eye on Alexandra and almost slipped off the curb before toddling quickly to catch up with the others.

Alexandra sighed, looked at the fork and followed Billy's advice.

And up a bending street, Alexandra found her inheritance. The Wider World occupied a former theatre of the same name. Though the stage hadn't been used in years, the bookstore endured. The fussy Victorian architecture and darkened marquee sprawling across the building facade gave the store a sort of antiquated European air. It was a building that any reasonable person loved immediately and Alexandra, being exceptionally reasonable, couldn't be happier.

Alexandra's luggage was stacked neatly at the front door—the entirety of her life packed into a suitcase, a makeup case, and a garment bag. She thought of the last time she'd been in her aunt's presence. It was a family gathering, everyone at her grandparents'; packed into cots and doubled-up in small beds, children giggling their little conspiracies against parents who tried to set aside old grievances while sharing bracingly sweet wine.

Her aunt, Tabitha, was as gregarious as Alexandra's grandfather and they bickered over politics and laughed over stories of broken bones and shattered hearts. Alexandra was young then, perhaps six, and adored them both. One had been to a war, the other had been to Antarctica. They'd led lives so big and so different from each other's.

That night, Tabitha announced she was going on another grand adventure, something about fighting whalers in the Pacific.

"Tabby," Grandmother said. "You can't live your entire life on the water."

"Oh, don't you tempt me, mother. I was born with sea legs. Land's the only place I've ever feared drowning. Give me a good boat and an enthusiastic wind, and I'll sail until the sun consumes the earth."

This sounded like a superb life to Alexandra. When she was finally herded towards bed with her younger sister and all the rest of the cousins, Alexandra saw the seven seas in her dreams. Glistening water, endless blue skies, frolicking sea life, and treacherous storms.

Oh, and pirates! There must be pirates!

The next day her grandfather said something cruel to her aunt, something about motherhood and duty. Alexandra didn't catch it all, but did hear the yelling, the family separating them both. There was a darkness in her aunt's eyes as she walked off into the countryside, and Alexandra feared she'd never return.

Daydreams of sailing followed, then a plan. Alexandra retreated from her family, slipped upstairs to the room she shared with four others, then packed one small backpack. She raided the kitchen for provisions, then stole away to grandfather's pier to untie the lone rowboat. Her younger sister had picked up her trail at some point and appeared right before Alexandra shoved off. Her little sister begged her way on board. Even if Alexandra had only packed food for one, there would be plenty of glory to go around, so Alexandra helped her four-year-old sister down into the boat. An hour later, her aunt swam out across the pond to recover the boat, now adrift without its oars.

The entire family gathered at the shore as Tabitha saw to retrieve the boat and tow it back to the pier. Alexandra was humiliated.

"A noble attempt," her aunt told her.

Alexandra cleared tears from her face, then said "Next time."

"Next time," her aunt agreed. "But maybe try a body of water that actually reaches the ocean."

Young Alexandra nodded wisely.

Until that moment, while all her earthly possessions were stacked against the door of the Wider World Book & Novelties, Alexandra had forgotten the long trails of mascara tears on her mother's face as she watched the rowboat return to the pier. She'd forgotten the stony silence between Tabitha and the rest of the family. Alexandra remembered how unfair it felt for Tabitha to be blamed.

Alexandra's grandfather asked Tabitha to go. Which she did, and far further than anyone in the family expected. She'd never visit or call or write ever again.

"You made your mother believe you'd both drowned," her father explained later as they sat alone in the guest bedroom. "It's our duty to protect you and your sister and we failed you both. It's also your duty to protect your sister."

The young Alexandra now understood the duty of love, but her bold heart was not done with adventure.

When she considered studying abroad, it took her parents months to convince her that Chile would be too far from home and from her sister, who needed Alexandra's steadying presence. When Alexandra considered a career in investigative journalism, her parents argued that she'd encounter far too many untrustworthy people and that the smarter choice would be accounting.

"It will all fall to you," her mother said. "When your father and I are gone, you'll need to be ready because your sister will depend on you."

When Alexandra met the pediatrician in her former life, her parents applauded her choice of an admirable and true companion, a man who worked doggedly to create security for himself and for her. The pediatrician feared the chaos of his own childhood infecting their home, so built a protective wall of wealth and order. He lived up to his duty to her so she vowed to live up to her duty to him.

She could not match his zealous work ethic, though, and often found herself alone in their large, empty home filling her time with books of adventure and mystery. He gently mocked the stories, but Alexandra also wondered if he feared them. If he feared the danger they brought within his protective walls.

Then her sister called, desperate. The pediatrician refused to open their home to her.

"We don't know what your sister will bring with her," the pediatrician said. "But we can rent her a place until she gets back on her feet. That will be better for everyone."

Her sister was five years dead by the time Alexandra received the letter from the executor of her aunt's estate. Alexandra and her sister should've bought a boat and set out to find their aunt on one of her mysterious and thrilling adventures. Instead, Alexandra had allowed herself to become entombed by duty and love.

This was why she fled the pediatrician. This was why she brought so little with her. At first, she was confused as to why her aunt, who was born with sea legs, would be anchored to a bookstore in a small town. But the sea was *right there*. Within minutes of locking the front door, her aunt could be in a boat and out into the infinite. The ocean was *right there*.

Alexandra realized now what her aunt saw in this town, in this life, and had a hope for what it could offer her—a port from which she could disembark at any time she chose and in any direction her destiny might shine.

"Hallo," a voice called from behind. Alexandra turned, scanned the street, but found no one.

"Up here, mum," the voice called, drawing her eyes up the balcony of a narrow, three-story Tudor building. There sat an old man in a ratty newsboy cap, rocking gently in a wicker chair. "Just keeping an eye on yer things, you know.

We don't have thieves in this town, but Mrs. Fastly felt ye'd appreciate some honest eyes on yer bags."

"Oh, thank you," Alexandra said, waving up to the man. "My name's Alexandra."

"Reeves," the old man called back, then pushed himself up off the rocking chair, taking a moment to steady, then stretched out his back. "You got your auntie's glimmer about ya."

"Oh. I do?"

"Seems to me. What kinda fish do ye like, mum? We'll bring you a meal on the morrow."

"Oh, I'm not sure," Alexandra said. "That's very kind. Just surprise me."

The man nodded, then turned for the door.

"Oh, Mr. Reeves?" Alexandra called.

The old man turned back.

"Just Reeves, mum."

"Yes, okay. Do you know the man with the office at the top of the hill?"

The old man smiled. "I do."

"I met him but didn't catch his name."

"Not surprising."

"Oh," Alexandra. "So, do you know it? And do you know what he does with all those little cards?"

"He holds the town together, mum," Reeves said, then turned back for the door.

"What's that mean?" Alexandra asked. "And what's his name?"

But Reeves now spoke loudly to someone inside his home, "You're right, she's a looker! Don't know much about seafood, though!"

"Oh, we can fix something else!" a female voice called back loudly. "Did ye offer her some of my shepherd's pie! We always hear such nice things about the shepherd's pie!"

"That we do, but didn't think of it until now!"

"If the lass is still out there, ask her about the shepherd's pie!"

The old man closed the door, yet the loud voices still seeped out into the night. "Poor thing's just arrived into town, dearie! Doesn't need us haranguing her over her dining preferences, you know!"

She could hear the voices descending from the third floor to the second floor.

"It's a lovely shepherd's pie, Reeves!"

"It's a dandy, that shepherd's pie! No one's arguing with you! Everyone agrees, it's a right dandy shepherd's pie! She said 'surprise me,' and maybe we can surprise her with a shepherd's pie or maybe we surprise her with a nice cod filet! We can think on it and decide on the morrow!"

"On the morrow, then."

"Yes, dearie."

Lights flicked on in the second floor.

"But when she said 'Surprise me,' was she saying 'surprise me with something fish-like,' or 'surprise me with anything.'?"

"Don't know, dearie! Didn't ask!"

"You're lucky you still got yer good looks, Reeves!"

"I know it!"

"Did she ask about The Man?"

"She did!"

"Oh! What'd she say?"

"Oh, no," Alexandra said, blushing and quickly kicking her luggage out of the way of the front door. The deadbolt resisted her key, but finally yielded with a slight squeal. The old wood had swelled from the damp night, and it took a firm shoulder to nudge it open. A gentle "ding" sounded from a tiny, brass bell hanging overhead. Inside, the familiar dusty smell of a bookstore greeted her. Millions of pages, slowly yellowing and shedding fibers into the air. Stories of love, war, adventure, and intrigue waited on tall, wooden bookshelves arranged in a labyrinth as dense and daunting as the human dramas they recounted. There were no signs to point the way to where one might find science fiction or picture books or memoirs. It was all just shelves, books, and the assumption that the right book would find the right person at the right time. Alexandra could die amid the maze and not be found for weeks.

"I could hide from him here," Alexandra whispered to herself, thinking of the Man Who Held The Town Together. "I could hide from love and pluck my heart from my chest, stuff it into one of these books, never to be found. That would be the safe thing to do."

But her heart fluttered sadly, hurt by Alexandra's careless disregard.

"Oh, behave," she told her heart. "You know that I am only teasing you."

Alexandra pulled her luggage inside, leaned against the door so that the deadbolt could catch and lock. Facing the store, she scanned the crammed shelves and narrow walkways again, seeing if she could make better sense of how the shop was laid out.

But no, it seemed ordered by a map that had lived and died with her aunt. The disorder unsettled Alexandra and she envisioned a staggering campaign of assessing and re-ordering that would surely consume her life for the weeks and months to follow.

But not today, she thought. She walked to the back of the store towards a set of double doors leading into the main theatre. She pulled at the handles, but they held, locked. She tested her key in the deadbolt, but it didn't fit.

"Bother," she said.

She wound her way to a spiral staircase near the back. It led to the balcony, now a partially-exposed loft. The stairs creaked and swayed slightly as she ascended. Upstairs, more books served as walls, shielding from the public eye a rickety iron bed, a cherrywood chifferobe, and a matching chest of drawers. She sat on the bed, listening to the springs and frame groan like an old mutt woken on a cold, winter morning.

She checked a side table for any other keys that might unlock the theatre. She crossed to the kitchenette, looking for a hook or a small plate or little box, anything that might contain the other half of her inheritance.

Then she spied a piece of masking tape stuck on the wall with "SIGN" written on it in black magic marker. Below it, a light switch. Alexandra smiled and hurried across the room, flicking on the light. She sped down the staircase as it groaned under her weight. She darted through the shelves and burst out the front door. She backed into the street, gazing up at the vibrant reds, greens, and whites of the glowing marquee. Alexandra giggled, clapped her hands together, and wondered at her future.

"She found the lightswitch, Reeves!" a voice called from across the street.

"That she did, dearie!"

In The Town Where All Things Are Possible,

the Man Who Held The Town Together yearned for human touch with a widower's conflicted sorrow. Every brush of another person's fingertips brought with it a burst of euphoria, followed by a chill of regret.

It's been years, The Man reminded his ravaged heart.

An arm fell over The Man's shoulders unexpectedly as he sat near the empty skating rink lit up by towering floodlights. The Man Who Held the Town Together turned to see Alexandra and felt his body awaken, his heart flutter and stretch. His face warmed, his fingertips tremored. Finally a shaky smile.

"I'll be," Alexandra said, looking out at the rink circled by a wooden rail. It stood where downtown gave way to a humble forested park. Upon arriving, she'd expected to find the entire town's population packed onto the ice, but it was only the strange man with no name.

"I still don't understand it," she said, leaning on The Man Who Held The Town Together as if they were two old pals admiring a natural wonder.

Then Alexandra remembered they weren't old pals and managed a clumsy laugh while pulling her arm off his shoulder. Despite the enormity of the task, The Man Who Held The Town Together forced his eyes up to meet Alexandra's.

"The fried pies should be along shortly," The Man said.

Alexandra's smile bloomed, mystified and thoroughly pleased. She then nodded her approval while saying "that'll be fine," as if conducting a bit of business. "So, where is everybody?"

The Man Who Held The Town Together stepped toward the ice rink, placing his hands on the waist-high railing with wooden barrier boards. He inspected the freshly resurfaced ice.

"Perhaps they weren't in the mood to skate tonight," he said, then looked back at her. "The rink is open year-round, after all."

"How do you keep the ice frozen through the summer?"

The Man leaned down on one knee and motioned for her to join him. He placed his palm on the concrete and she did the same. A painful chill shocked her palm. Alexandra flinched her hand away. She tested it again, noticing the air wasn't cold near the concrete, but below freezing right on the concrete's surface.

"How?"

"We don't know," The Man said, shrugging. "It's only here, in this small part of town. We don't know what else to do about the chill, so we built an ice rink over it."

Alexandra shook her head. She stood up and the man followed.

"So, is the twist ending that we were dead all along?" she asked.

"I feel pretty alive, don't you?"

A moment passed.

"I do," she said, their eyes growing more comfortable in each other's company.

The Man led Alexandra to a long wooden cabinet with numerous cubby holes containing ice skates of all sizes. She found a scuffed pair of white leather skates in her size.

She ran her fingers over tufts of pink fur that sprouted out the top of the inside lining. A pink and blue lightning bolt shot from heel to toe.

"I saw a pair like this when I was a child and begged my mom to buy them for me," Alexandra said. "And they're right here. In my size."

She looked at The Man.

"Do you just get used to this sort of thing happening all the time?" she asked.

"No. And I hope I never do."

Alexandra plucked the skates from the cubby and carried them to the small metal bleachers that faced the rink. She sat and unzipped her leather boots, then sat them next to the bench. The Man Who Held The Town Together joined her to tie on his own pair of ice skates—simple brown leather with a sunburst emblazoned on each skate.

"I like that logo," Alexandra said, feeling the thread with the tip of her finger. "What's it for?"

"It's . . ." the Man began, considering. "I'm actually not sure. The people who built the town used it a lot, so I guess it's like our crest or something."

"Do towns have crests?" Alexandra asked.

The Man only shrugged as he laced on the skates. Alexandra made a decision, then looked directly at The Man.

"What's your name?" Alexandra asked.

The Man turned to her to answer, but he hesitated, frowning.

"Ahem," a voice called from behind.

They turned to see Mrs. Milda Gratherson leaning against her walker. A handsome and bearded middle-aged man in a paint-splattered shirt and carpenter pants stood next to her, holding a small plate of fried pies. A few steps behind them was a tall brunette woman in a black-and-gold Victorian dress with a gold-and-silver mask strapped across the right side of her face, embedded with gears and tiny metallic flourishes, hiding her right eye. She thought of the strange contraption in The Man's tiny office, guessing that the same tinkerer had made the mask.

"We've brought you some nibblings," Mrs. Gratherson said. "Did you find your store all right?"

"I did, thank you," Alexandra said. "The shop is quite . . . well, I've got my work cut out for me, I think."

"Your aunt had her own way of doing things," the woman in the mask said. "I'll try to make it by soon. It took me years to get my head around her idea of order, so perhaps I can help."

"That'd be lovely."

"And my son, Gabriel, is also happy to help," Mrs. Gratherson said, elbowing the large man with a bushy beard and bright blue eyes.

"At the very least, I know which way to face a hammer," he said, revealing a beaming, toothy smile beneath his beard.

Mrs. Gratherson motioned for Gabriel to lay the plate down on the bleachers. As he did, Alexandra looked back at the strange woman in the mask. The design was delicate and ornate. The gears ticked, but served no obvious purpose. The mask was surprising and beautiful, and would've been eerie if not for the woman's kind smile. The trio waved and retreated from the ice rink.

"Um, thank you!" Alexandra called and Mrs. Gratherson took a moment to wave again before clicking her walker off into the night.

Alexandra glanced at The Man Who Held The Town Together suspiciously.

"You suckered me into a date, didn't you?" she asked.

"Me? No." He gestured around them, at the humble brownstones and small shops, at the cobblestone pathways and ornate lamp posts. "But this town has its own ideas."

Alexandra belted out a sharp laugh. "Okay, enough of that. Let's skate."

Alexandra pushed herself up onto the rubber blade covers of the skates. The Man followed and they took small steps toward the door to the ice rink. He unlatched it, swung it open. He slid off the protectors, one at a time, stepping onto the ice, then held his hand out to Alexandra. She arched an eyebrow, shed the blade protectors, then zipped onto the ice. She whisked away, launching into a graceful sprint, rounding the small rink, then carving the ice in a hockey stop, spreading snow out toward The Man.

"I think I'm the one who got suckered," he said, then closed the door behind him.

Alexandra bolted away and he chased after. She hopped to turn herself towards The Man while still skating back-wards, teasing as he failed to keep pace.

"Can you believe I've never skated before?" Alexandra asked.

"No," The Man called between heaving breaths. "As a matter of fact—I don't believe that—at all."

Alexandra laughed, hopped back around, then spun into

a tight, fast pirouette before losing her footing and crashing to the ice. She smiled broadly as she slid, back flat on the ice, in slow lazy circles.

"Are you okay?" The Man called, finally catching up to her.

"Oh, yes!" She gasped in heavy breaths. "When I get to know you better, I'll tell you all about my illustrious career as a shut-down defender for my high school hockey team."

"Pretty good?" The Man asked, easing down onto the ice to lie on his back beside her.

"My sister was better," Alexandra said. "She was clever, I was angry. We made a good team."

The Man didn't pry, which she appreciated. The stars were clear above them. The sweet scent of fried pies beckoned.

He eased up onto his skates, then held out his hands. She smiled, nodded, then held up her hands to be helped up. He took them, but she yanked him down to the ice on top of her. It was a clumsy, laughing moment while he struggled to push up onto his hands. They were fully within each other's gazes and the world was empty around them.

"It expects us to kiss, doesn't it?" she asked. "Your town with all its ideas."

His mouth opened in reply, but he found himself suddenly incapable of speech. Her hand moved to his cheek, giving him a crooked smile.

"Not yet."

She pushed away from him, sliding on her back on the ice, then deftly rolling onto her skates and speeding away. He laughed, his voice clear and weightless for the first time in years. He pushed to his feet and gave chase, both of them thoroughly absorbed in the novelty of a fresh romance.

They skated deep into the night, following one another in careless circles, never touching, yet trapped in orbit.

Where memories are hidden

In The Town Where All Things Are Possible,

an astonishing poster appeared years ago in the narrow alleyway between the tavern and the grocery mart. It stretched five feet wide by two and a half feet tall. Rather than a static image, the poster displayed a thirty-second loop of a tall woman in a flowing gold and green ballgown and long, auburn curls waving orange construction flags while dancing down an abandoned, pockmarked street surrounded by depressed, industrial buildings. The words "Gisela Cook" glittered in the top right corner in towering, glamorous, silver letters like an obscure perfume ad.

The angle of the camera was high, potentially shot from the roof of a building. The buildings were damaged and derelict, as if they'd barely survived a war. A single burning black tire sent a dense black plume high into the sky. At the end of the loop, a man burst from the bottom right corner, sprinting after the dancer. This new figure wore a blue-and-red-patched hunting coat, a black-brimmed hat, and carried an object at his side.

The hunter's urgency frightened Alexandra as she gazed upon the magical poster. Just as the hunter was about to collide with the dancer, the image broke to static, then restarted the loop.

She'd ventured out from the bookshop that morning after searching the tiny kitchenette to find only a congealed bottle of mustard and a fistful of sugar packets of uncertain provenance. On her way to the town's modest grocery story, she'd discovered the aging, glossy poster while wandering the winding streets and alleyways. She ignored her growling stomach as she lifted a curled-up corner of the poster to peer behind it to see if a television screen was cleverly hidden beneath, but she found only a brick wall. The paper felt slick and unremarkable, like a normal poster. She waved her hand in front of it to see if there was a projection coming from behind her, but no. The video seemed to be embedded in the paper, an eternal loop of the beautiful, happy dancer and her sudden and mysterious predator.

She noticed a small sunburst logo in the very bottom right corner of the poster, its beams animated, sending little yellow lines out in all directions that faded inches from the sun. She'd seen the same logo on The Man's skates.

"It is too early in the morning for such sad things," a voice called down the alley.

Alexandra turned to see a squat, olive-skinned man with a wiry black mustache that partially hid his smile. A starched white apron hung over his tan slacks. His t-shirt read "Go With Greek" in a sharp, eccentric font.

"Come," the man said with a warm smile, waving her with him as he disappeared around the alley toward the grocery mart.

Alexandra's eyes returned to the moving image on the poster, studying the way the woman danced joyfully. *No, not joyfully*, Alexandra decided. *Defiantly*.

The hunter emerged from the corner of the poster, sprinting, wielding something. *A gun? A hammer? Something terrible*, Alexandra thought.

She sighed, then followed after the stranger in the apron. She turned the corner, venturing one last gaze, hoping that the loop would suddenly stretch further in time so Alexandra could learn the dancer's fate. But the Town held its secret close.

In The Town Where All Things Are Possible,

there lived a Greek shop owner who sang pop music loudly and without shame while his customers explored the aisles of his small, cramped grocery mart. There was no accompaniment by radio, record player, or even musicbox. Just the man's bellowing voice, the chimes of a cash register, and the clink of bottles being restocked on shelves.

The un-air-conditioned store was packed with nuts, rice, dry pasta, and grains of all kinds kept in crates that were open to the world. Along the walls were shelves tightly packed with bottles of wine, juice, beer, and milk, but without the traditional labeling pleading for attention. Instead, strips of brown tape proclaimed each bottle's contents and volume, with a price written hastily in black ink. It was a store frozen in the 1800s in all ways aside from the singing Greek and a framed Smiths album hanging above the looming cast-iron cash register. The washed-out orange record cover depicted a weary woman leaning heavily on her hand, a cigarette dangling between her fingers.

Alexandra sat on a narrow wire-frame chair at a small bistro table tucked as far into the corner as possible. At the moment that Alexandra bit into the delicate and plump flesh of a roma tomato, the Greek began belting out Depeche Mode's "Enjoy the Silence," his eyes closed, pausing now and then as long instrumental parts played out in his head. The grocer was enveloped by the song, even as he rang up orders or led a mother with a wailing child to the backstock of diapers.

As the song lilted into sorrow, Alexandra feared the Greek grocer would begin crying. An adult crying in public was high among the sights that most horrified Alexandra. As the Greek's voice wavered and caught, clearly from the song unearthing some heavy, precious memory, he and Alexandra were alone in the store. If this grown man crumbled, Alexandra would be forced to act.

Then the Greek took a deep breath and cleared a tear that had fallen from his eye into his mustache. He then began nodding his head to something more uptempo, a rhythm pumping only within mind. He danced as he restocked paper bags.

Alexandra turned her focus to the modest plate of olives, tomatoes, and smoked salmon, with a little dipping bowl filled with a lemon and pepper sauce the Greek had whipped up.

When the Greek began singing, she quickly recognized the lyrics of "Karma Chameleon" by Culture Club. When he reached the line:

Loving would be easy if your colors were like my dreams.
Red, Gold, and Green.
Red, Gold, and Gre–en,

the Greek wavered, sat down heavily on a stool that creaked like the sigh of an old woman. He stared at his hands. She couldn't know what the song had knocked loose within him, but she also felt something knock loose in herself. Her sister and her mother singing over breakfast while Alexandra and her father plugged their ears. Alexandra put down the tomato and hugged herself tight, holding in the heartache that threatened to break through the stitches.

The silence was too much for Alexandra, the spaces in the air filling too quickly with other things, so she forced herself to speak.

"Do you have anything that is easy to cook?" Alexandra called to the Greek. His eyes lifted in wide confusion, as if she'd pulled him from a deep sleep.

"No," he answered.

"The thing is, I have no real kitchen," Alexandra explained, walking to the counter. "I have a hot plate and a microwave. I live in a bookstore."

"Ah," the Greek replied, chewing over the problem. "This is not a problem. One moment."

The Greek placed his meaty hands onto the counter and pushed himself off the stool.

"Gerald!" he hollered at a wooden door behind the cash register. "Boy! You are needed!"

"It's not urgent," Alexandra said, worried about the wheels that had just been put into motion. "I think I'm having lunch with my across-the-street neighbors."

The Greek faced Alexandra, smiled wide beneath the black, bushy mustache. "Yes, Mrs. Reeves's shepherd's pie is wonderful."

He then began cooing "Famous Blue Raincoat" softly, as if soothing a fussy baby. Alexandra smiled, wary, then retreated back to her bistro table to escape the moment. The wooden door swung wide and a short young man emerged, his face sprouting a wiry beard that raced out in all directions like a supernova.

Once Gerald saw Alexandra, his eyes went wide. "You!" Gerald said.

Alexandra glanced around, though she knew she was the only customer in the store. She turned back to Gerald, but could think of nothing to say.

"One moment!" Gerald said, then slipped back through the swinging door.

Alexandra turned to the Greek for an answer, but he only sang:

> *I guess that I miss you, I guess I forgive you*
> *I'm glad you stood in my way.*

Rushed footsteps preceded the door bursting open again, banging against the wall, spilling pecans that clacked across the floor. Gerald now carried a large leather portfolio as the Greek launched into "Walk This Way"—the Run DMC version—in a syrupy lounge tradition. Gerald waved Alexandra to follow him outside the store. Without a plan on how to remove herself from the situation, she followed.

Outside, Gerald walked quickly around the store back to the alley with the poster of the defiant dancer, still stuck in her tragic loop. Gerald spun to face Alexandra, who paused at the corner of the alley. He motioned her close with a nervous, desperate smile. She approached, but kept a comfortable distance.

"I am so glad you are here!" he whispered. "I asked for you, and I knew you would come!"

"I don't understand what is happening," Alexandra said, keeping two steps between them. "I just need some food for my place."

"Yes, yes, yes, I will cook for you and bring it to the bookstore!" Gerald said happily, then unzipped the portfolio. "I need you to see something first!"

Alexandra took a half step backwards, her eyes on the portfolio, her arms raising up in instinctive defense. Gerald saw her hesitation.

"Oh, um, no, it is nothing for you to, um, be afraid of!" Gerald said. "I am, just, I'm sorry, I'm really nervous and I just, there's no one else, you see, there's no one else I can talk to because, you must understand, there's no one else that can see these because, as you know, we all live here. And you live here too, now, finally, but not in the same way. You will see these in a way that no one else can, all these people, do you understand? Well, it's hard to explain, but you will know when you see them."

The young man worked on the knotted band wrapped around the portfolio. "Tell me, have you met the most beautiful woman in the world? Her name is Tessa? Please tell me you've met her! I mean, no, actually, please tell me you haven't met her, because maybe that's better!"

Gerald watched her with an intensity Alexandra could not comprehend, never quite settling his eyes on any one part of her face. She now understood the intensity was not directed at her, but at his pain. That was something she could understand.

"I don't know, maybe I've met her," Alexandra said. "I don't remember the name."

Gerald held the portfolio toward her.

"May I show you?" he asked.

Alexandra hesitated taking the portfolio.

"Am I going to see something I don't want to see?" she asked.

"No!" Gerald said, then catching her meaning. "No. No. No. I don't do those kinds of drawings. No. You'll see! You'll see Tessa, but not—no, no, no, not in that way!"

Alexandra sighed, knowing the only way through was forward. She took the portfolio and slowly opened it. Dozens of large, loose sheets of Bristol paper fluttered as the portfolio yawned open. On the top sheet was an image of the woman from the night before, a metallic contraption strapped to the right side of her face, covering one eye. With what looked to be a million, tiny pen scratches, her face was perfectly captured, every little gear and screw in the contraption realized in vivid detail. Stunned, Alexandra ventured a look up to the expectant Gerald. He motioned for her to continue.

She flipped to another sheet, this one equally lush and exact, but of the woman from head to toe, wearing a black Victorian dress, looking away, the contraption almost out of sight. More sheets revealed the woman, and only the woman, looking away—pained, distant, captured perfectly, but unknowable.

"These are excellent," Alexandra finally said, closing the portfolio and retying the band. She handed it back to Gerald who quickly stuffed the portfolio under his arm as if it possessed dire secrets. "And, yes, I've seen her. Why do you need me to see these, Gerald?"

"Thank you, I mean, well, thank you. The others would misunderstand them. You see, they know her and I too well, and of course, she can never see them because they would make her feel, well, oh God, you must understand!"

"They would make her uncomfortable?" Alexandra asked.

"Yes! Yes! Yes!" he said, hopping excitedly. "That's it! I knew you would understand! I knew the town sent you to me!"

"But why?" Alexandra asked. "I still don't know what you expect of me."

"Just to see," Gerald said, suddenly calming as he cradled the portfolio. "To see and understand. I've been alone with these drawings for too long."

He closed his eyes, focused on his breath, his energy evaporated and he was calm.

"I'm sorry if I scared you," he said. "People say I should be calm and of course they're right. It's just all my fault, all my fault. I fumbled her love like an over-excited child. I wish I'd known." Gerald now spoke only to the ground. "Why don't they tell us how to manage something as unwieldy as love?"

Alexandra smiled, nodded. "I don't know, but they should."

He looked up, his eyes sweeping the poster, then finding Alexandra.

"I'm not normally like this, you know," Gerald said. "Or I wasn't before. It's the pain, you see."

"I do. Your drawings are wonderful, but yes, don't show them to her. It'll only make things harder for you both."

Alexandra wasn't certain that was the right advice, but she figured it would at least do no harm. She looked behind him, toward the poster just as the hunter neared the dancer, a moment before the loop returned to the beginning.

"What can you tell me about this?" she asked, pointing.

Gerald watched the happy dancer, then the sudden predator. Gerald sighed and turned from the end, knowing it well.

"It's proof that, even here, not all things are truly possible."

Alexandra frowned. She disliked riddles and also wondered if she'd come to dislike the town.

"What can you tell me about the man who works on the hill?" Alexandra asked. "Why won't anyone tell me his name?"

Gerald arched a clever eyebrow. "He believes he holds the town together and he's even worse off than me, if you can believe it. We all worry for him, that he will work himself to death just like The Men who came before him."

"But what exactly does he do?"

"No one knows. Someone like him has always been in the town, working to an early grave on a task only he and his mentor understand. But we do know that without them, our town suffers."

He glanced back down to his portfolio, patting it proudly.

"Thank you for looking. Now, go back to The Wider World and I'll bring you lunch, then dinner until fate and fortune gifts you a kitchen."

"I don't have much money," Alexandra said. "And I think my neighbors are bringing me something today. They said 'on the morrow' but I'm not exactly sure if that means lunch or dinner or next week."

Gerald chuckled. "Her shepherd's pie is divine. I'll bring you something you can eat whenever you need it and no money. I only need your eyes." Gerald held up the portfolio.

"Gerald!" the Greek shouted from next door. "Where are you?"

"Only your eyes," he sang, then danced to a song only he could hear, waltzing out of the alleyway and back to his family store.

"Gerald!" Alexandra called.

His head popped back into view.

"Drawing her over and over again," Alexandra said, "I don't know if that is healthy for you or for her."

"I know," Gerald said. "I've thought the same thing, but . . . the drawing helps."

His smile brightened. "How about this? You are new here, so I will draw you the town. To help you understand."

Alexandra smiled. "But I don't think anyone can really understand this town."

"That's true! That's true!" Gerald said with eyes as wide as moons. "Isn't it so wonderful?"

The delicate art of bookselling

In The Town Where All Things Are Possible,

Alexandra realized she had no idea how to run a bookstore, so decided to just unlock the door to see what tumbled in. She'd attempted to decipher her aunt's ordering system, but she found sea-faring tales nestled on shelves next to contemporary romances, decades-old technology journals side by side with parenting how-tos, gardening primers woven within magical realism.

And with her aunt gone, Alexandria wondered if all there was to do was tip over every shelf, pile the books up into the center of the store, and begin reshelving by her own system. *Probably, yes, that is exactly what I need to do. But not today.*

Instead, she threw back the deadbolt and took a deep breath. *The more books I sell, the fewer I'll have to sort through later.*

The excited sea winds pushed the door open, then ruffled pages, unsettled dust, and explored every nook of the store. Alexandra shouldered the door closed again. She took a moment to admire a sign with a whale opening up its mouth to swallow a boat. Beside the boat was the word "OPEN." She flipped it over to see the whale chomping down on the boat along with the word "CLOSED".

Across the street, Reeves watched from his balcony, giving Alexandra a thumbs up.

Alexandria turned to the task of tidying up the shop and to see what clues she might find on the business of book-buying, book-selling, and general retail best practices. She began uncovering sticky notes and napkins with her aunt's looping, carefree handwriting. Some messages with quick math equations absent context, others addresses with no attributed names, book titles with cryptic question marks after. These were her aunt's unknowable inner-workings leaking out one rushed note at a time.

She then found a recipe box stuffed to bursting. Inside were names and simple descriptions:

Jonathan: handsome chin and kind eyes, but gaunt (sick?), fading memory (remember the list of what he's already bought so he doesn't buy it again)

- *Westerns,*
- *Presidential bios (don't engage!)*
- *Old, ugly wars*

Milda: keep walkway clear for her walker, piercing blue eyes

- *Bodice rippers*
- *Female-centered history*
- *German philosophy*
- *Don't trust with secrets!!!*

Wendy: brunette with the most interesting eyeglasses, what a nose!, librarian(give discount)

- *Contemporary fiction*
  - *Unusual protagonists*
- *Fantasy*
  - *Dragons*
  - *No swords or necromancy*

Tessa: lovely mask and where does she get those old dresses?, don't ask about Gerald

- *Poetry*
- *Astrophysics*
- *Anything set in Scotland*

Gerald: son of Basil and Calliope, works at grocer, <u>Don't Ask About Tessa!</u>
Graphic Novels

- *Drawing techniques*
- *Ancient history w/ pictures*

"A Rosetta Stone!" Alexandra said, then dug through the box for a name that might fit the Man Who Held The Town Together. But first she found:

Connor Reeves: goes by his last name, bushy eyebrows and a wart above his eyes, nosy and likes his pipe, but knows his books(ask for reccs)

- *Mid-century mysteries*
- *Sports*
  - *Football (Not American)*
  - *Boxing*
  - *Anything else as long as it's "clever"*

Róisín Reeves: Wild curls, SO TALL, always remembers everyone's birthdays, willing to help watch the store, don't ask her opinion unless you really want it, Shepherd's Pie!!!

- *Exotic cookbooks*
- *Scifi*
  - *Character-focused*

- *Poetry, but only if it's sad or mostly about trees*

"Connor and Róisín," Alexandra said, trying to commit their names to memory.

She flipped through more cards with names of those she'd yet to meet. Nothing on the man in question. She shelved the cards to return to later, then found a mug shaped like two cats reading back-to-back on a porch swing, which surfaced a memory of her aunt wearing a cat-themed sweater. The cats were skiing. There might have been a pun involved.

Alexandra studied the mug, then looked around the shop, thinking about how her younger self would've been so delighted with excavating books from amid all the towering chaos. *Why hadn't my parents ever brought me here?*

Alexandra knelt down to dig through more clutter, then thought she heard the bell, but when she straightened, the store was empty. She bent back down to look more, finding a yellow notepad with numbers all adding up to 2,508. She flipped the pages and, though the numbers in the equation differed, they always added up to 2,508.

She thought she heard something rustling, so she straightened, mug and notepad in hand. There stood the town seamstress just across the counter.

Alexandra gasped and the mug tumbled upwards from her grip. The seamstress caught the mug calmly, then sat it down on the counter.

"Oh!" Alexandra said.

The seamstress, a thin, serious woman, lifted her nose slightly so she could look at Alexandra through the bottom of her bifocals.

"I am not much of a reader," the seamstress said. "But I am glad that you're here."

"Oh, um, thank you. My name's Alexandra. And you are?"

"Elena," she said, sliding a business card across the desk. "I am a seamstress."

The card read only:

Elena
I Am A Seamstress

"Oh, thank you," Alexandra flipped the card over, but the back was empty. "Nice to meet you . . ." She flipped it back to the front. "Elena. I don't currently have any clothes that need mending but I'll let you know." Alexandra flipped the card back over to make sure she didn't overlook the contact info. She did not because it simply wasn't there. She flipped the card over once more, because surely . . . yet no. "Somehow."

"You are kind, I can tell these things," Elena said, then swept out the door, jingling the brass bell as she closed the door behind her and strode down the street.

The sea winds burst in again, the door swinging wide. The open sign clattered.

"Goodness, this won't do," Alexandra said.

Alexandra rounded the register to reach for the door. From somewhere within the town, a piano played jauntily. She listened for a few moments, then closed the door again, firm. She turned to resume her work, but the door swept open once again, bell ringing. Just at that moment, a tall, broad-shouldered man walked by. Stopped as he noticed the open door, then popped his head in. He possessed a magnificent beard of silver hair and curled locks flowing from under his wide-brimmed straw hat.

"You're open?" he asked, holding the door with a large hand roughened by years of difficult labor.

"Yes, I suppose I am," Alexandra said.

The man strode into the shop, took a moment to check his internal map, then pointed towards a back corner, following his own directions.

"Let me know if you need help," Alexandra called, then realizing she knew almost nothing about the store and would be of little help if help was needed.

Alexandra walked to the door, began to shut it, then changed her mind and left it wide open. The piano still played somewhere beyond.

"Hallo!" Connor Reeves called from across the street.

Alexandra looked back into the store for the silver-haired man, but saw only stacks of books. She stepped outside and looked up at Reeves sitting on his balcony.

"Hallo yourself," Alexandra said, shielding her eyes from the sun. "Your wife wouldn't happen to be named Róisín Reeves, would she?"

"That she would," Reeves called down. "Find our notecard, did ya?"

"I did. So, I think I'll be busy with the shop, but if you're still wanting to eat together, maybe you could just bring it over? If that's not too much trouble."

"Not at all, not at all. Let's make it lunch if you don't mind eating a mite early. The missus and I wake and sleep with the sun, so our clocks run differently than most others."

"That's fine, I'll see you soon."

Alexandra looked out across the town for the source of the piano, but couldn't see much past the brownstones shoulder to shoulder against one another. Beyond loomed the twin mountains and beyond them, the endless sea.

She checked the latch of the door to see if she could determine why it wouldn't stay shut. She saw some scoring on the brass from decades of use, but nothing obvious she could fix right away. She then sought out her customer. After some searching, she found him looking through a shelf with multiple volumes of Oscar Wilde, Jules Verne, Agatha Christie, and *Mad LIbs*.

"Finding everything all right?" she asked, dreading what would come if he said no.

"Yes, ma'am," he said, barely looking over from the shelves. "Just reorienting myself."

"I'll, umm, I'll leave you to it, then."

She returned to her register and pulled up the recipe box, thumbing through the cards until she came to:

Noah: ACTUAL SEA CAPTAIN!!!, more handsome than I can look at without proper eye protection—like the sun. Silver hair, strong, distracting hands, and oh those eyes! Likes stupid hats

- *Historical fiction*
- *Sometimes essays but I think he's trying to impress me*
- *Absolutely <u>nothing</u> about fishing*
- *Victorian sitting room dramas*

- *Jane Austen and the like*
  - *Soul mate?*

Asked me about my cat today, and I told him that Percy passed on, which made it quiet and weird; but that means something, right?

Went to the dock to get an eyeful of his ship. A modest trawler, but to the fish, it must be a leviathan. I could make myself invaluable, as there's no one in this town better at sea; but could I live as a fisherman? Haunting the same waters year in year out? I can clean a fish, but can I sail in circles?

Brought me a herring today. Still had its head attached. Very sweet but I gave the poor thing to Róisín. I just can't look my food in the eyes.

Over (Arrow)

Alexandra looked up to the store, feeling more than a little self-conscious. Noah the actual sea captain was nowhere to be seen. She flipped the card over.

Could he live with a vegetarian? I'm not sure how to feel him out on this? I lightly suggested a vegan cookbook to him just to gauge his reaction. He gave me nothing.

He's got another scar on his hand, on the palm. It was still angry and infected, but it should settle to a pink when alls said and done. Guessing it was a rope burn. Should've asked. Should've offered to put some ointment on it and he woulda let me, then the shop would've been quiet as my fingers worked over that massive paw, the calluses, the taught tendons. His eyes on me. Then he'd suggest flipping over the Open sign to Closed.

See next card.

"I don't think that I will, auntie," Alexandra said, putting the card back into the recipe box, closing it tight and stashing it deep within the shelf below the register. She wasn't certain she'd be able to look Noah the actual sea captain in the eyes ever again.

She dug out troves of indecipherable notes, damaged books, and wads of rubber bands. She swept it all into a trash can, which she would carry . . . where? Outside?

She sought out Noah, the actual sea captain and found him three rows deeper considering a well-worn copy of *Tess of the d'Urbervilles* and a notated *Emma Brown*. Picking up. Putting down. Picking up. Putting down. Not so much reading the books as feeling their weight in his hand, gauging their value by some mysterious metric known only to him. Perhaps this was also how he determined whether to toss a fish back into the sea.

Satisfied that he was doing fine without her, Alexandra left through the front door in search of a larger trash can. The bag jerked from her hand, startling her. A tall, knobby-kneed, dark-skinned teenager with a slight overbite of very bright white teeth sat on a bike right next to her. He tossed the bag into a garbage bin strapped to a trailer made out of bike wheels and a repurposed door. It was attached to his bright purple bike with customized gold swooping adornment so it seemed very plausible that, with the press of some discreet button, the bike would launch into space. He wore a red leather jacket and matching leather cap.

In short, the teenager was the most fantastic person she'd ever come across.

"Ma'am," the teen said, then leaned heavily on the

pedals to get his bike moving again. He tipped his cap as he continued along the street. "Ma'am."

Alexandra thought too late to ask if she was supposed to give him money or something.

"I'm ready if you are," Noah the actual sea captain called from inside the store.

"Yeah, sure," Alexandra said, hurrying in and around the counter.

Noah clomped a stack of six books down onto the counter. They ranged from a pulp fantasy adventure to essays on figurative drawing from the renaissance through cubism.

"Gonna be at sea awhile?" Alexandra asked.

"I'm sorry?"

Alexandra then felt like she'd just given away her aunt's secrets and blushed deeply. "Oh, just . . . you're a sailor, right?"

"I might be," Noah said, suspicious.

"So," Alexandra said, feeling as if she'd stepped in quicksand. "My aunt, she made notes on customers. She mentioned you were a sailor."

"I see. What else did she say about me?"

Alexandra shrugged, blushed as bright as a red sun, then mumbled "Nothing," in a way she hoped sounded like she actually meant "Nothing," but it was quite obvious it was the opposite of nothing. "I'm Alexandra, by the way."

"Noah," he said. "But you already knew that."

Noah studied Alexandra as she fumbled with the cash register. Hitting buttons, realizing they were the wrong buttons, then looking for other buttons to undo what she'd just done.

"Shoot," Alexandra finally said, taking the books, one at a time, to look for a cost.

"That one's used," Noah said. "Price is on the first page in pencil."

She flipped it. "Three dollars OBO?"

"Or best offer," Noah said. "But three dollars is fine."

Alexandra retrieved a note pad with an illustration of a cat in a big hat enjoying a tea party with Victorian mice. She wrote down the prices of each book, totaled it up. "I'll figure out this stupid register later," she said, and Noah peeled off cash from his money clip. He took the books in his large, distracting hands.

"Well," Noah said. "I hope whatever she wrote, it was nice. I thought a lot of her. She never said much—to me at least—but she ran a wonderful bookstore. It seemed like she never left."

"Never left? My aunt?" Alexandra asked. "The woman couldn't stay in one spot for more than a day, from how my dad talked about her."

"Hmm. Well, I've only seen her here the past five years since I resettled in this town. Perhaps she finally found her place."

This unsettled Alexandra for reasons she couldn't quite understand.

"At any rate, thank you for keeping it open." Noah looked out the window. "Storm's rolling in. If memory serves, your front door leaks and your aunt would have to jam towels against the door to keep the rain out. These books don't do well with water."

"Aye aye," Alexandra said, saluting. "I'll batten down the hatches."

Noah sighed, turned around, and left without another word.

A part of Alexandra's heart broke for her aunt's missed opportunity. She watched the one and only paying visitor hobble along the sidewalk—some old injury from braving an angry ocean and/or wrestling a kraken, Alexandra imagined.

As if summoned, the winds picked up, rustling books across the store.

"So, towels?" Alexandria asked herself while scanning the store.

A piece of paper slapped against the window and held it in place, the wind insisting on Alexandra's attention, so she peered closely. At first she thought the strange teenager collecting garbage had lost a part of his haul, but then she recognized the notecard. She hurried around the counter and out the front door, slapping her hand against the notecard as it wiggled like a beached fish. She held it up, reading over the careful, black-inked handwriting:

Randall Witherspoon
I Just Want To Live One More Day.

Alexandra searched the streets, looking for The Man Who Held The Town Together. Perhaps his cart had tipped over again, sending the cards swirling off like dervishes across the town. But no, the rogue card seemed to be the lone escapee.

"Or a carrier pigeon," Alexandra said, grinning.

"Hallo," Reeves called as he crossed the street, holding

a casserole dish. A very tall, thin woman with wild, brown curls followed, holding another covered dish.

"Oh, is it lunchtime already?" Alexandra asked. "And you must be Róisín?"

"That I am," Róisín said. "Did we catch you at a bad time, lass?"

Róisín then noticed the notecard in Alexandra's hands.

"That what I think it is?" Róisín asked.

"I think it is," Alexandra said.

Reeves smiled, then shooed her away. "Go on, we'll watch your shop for ye."

"That's okay," Alexandra said. "I can take it later."

"Oh, shush, you sweet thing," Róisín said. "Food'll keep till you get back and the mister and I don't have much else going today. It'll keep us out of trouble."

Alexandra turned to look towards the hill rising above the town. She smiled, waved, then hurried along the street.

"Oh!" Alexandra said, turning back to them. "The rains are coming and the door leaks, apparently."

"We know it," Róisín said, shooing her away.

Alexandra crossed the town, passing strangers who smiled warmly. The town was full of characters: a woman with a mouth-full of braces sporting hot pink bands which matched her blouse, a child wearing a space suit and pulling a cart full of spray cans, a thin man wearing a black duster while holding his bowler hat on his head with one hand and a poetry book in the other, shouting verse up at the approaching storm. She tried to match these curious strangers up with what she remembered from her aunt's notecards, but none seemed to fit. She'd need to study the cards more diligently.

The penguins marched by, trying to get home before the wind brought something more fierce. Billy nodded politely. Out across the sea, Alexandra saw the grey clouds rolling toward the town.

"My goodness, dear!" Wendy Fastly, the librarian, called while crossing Alexandra's path on the sidewalk. The ring of keys jingled at her waist where they were attached by a ribbon bow. "Get back inside before the heavens drop down upon us!"

"I am looking for the man with the notecards," Alexandra called back. "Do you know if he's at his office?"

"Of course he is, where else would he be?"

"I know this is silly, but I don't even know his name," Alexandra said.

The librarian smiled, then patted Alexandra's arm.

"Hurry," Wendy said, then walked on.

Alexandra rolled her eyes and muttered about state secrets.

"Oh!" Alexandra said, then turned to Wendy. "I need to figure out my aunt's shelving system but don't even know where to start."

"Sure, sure!" Wendy said, hurrying down the street while waving. "I'll come by when I can."

Alexandra pushed onwards. Within downtown, shops were shuttering their doors in preparation for the storm.

Clusters of fishermen emerged from a stone staircase leading down the cliffs. They held onto their hats while watching the clouds charge the town. Noah walked the opposite direction, holding his books in one arm and a grocery sack in the other. She could see Noah exchanging words with the fishermen and, it seemed to her, they were warning him away from the sea. Noah pushed on, as any proper actual sea captain would, and descended the stone steps.

Alexandra could see the small office perched on top, the light on. She quickened her pace.

At the foot of the hill, Alexandra saw Tessa minding a garden that grew almost untamed across the front yard of a very small house. At first glance, Alexandra assumed it was a Tudor miniature suitable only as a small shop, not as a place to live. Yet Alexandra saw through the open door a bed and a small stove. Tessa was moving the smaller potted plants inside her home while wearing another full-length Victorian dress—a bold blue with gold lacing. The fit was so snug that Tessa had to bend awkwardly to retrieve plants on the ground. It seemed odd to Alexandra to garden in such formal clothing, but everything in the town was odd in one way or another.

Tessa paused just long enough to offer Alexandra a welcoming smile, which Alexandra returned.

"Do you need help?" Alexandra called, but Tessa shook her head and gestured for Alexandra to continue her climb to The Man's office.

For a moment, Alexandra considered asking her about the heartbroken grocery shelf stocker, Gerald, but decided to leave the matter alone. She'd learned well enough that romantic entanglements were best left to the entangled, but it did seem meddling was a favored pastime for everyone else in the town. She turned to the hill, hoping that The Man was as dutiful as Wendy the librarian insisted so she could deliver the card and be on her way. Alexandra was certain she could still beat the storm if she was prudent.

Upon cresting the hill, she could see more of the ocean beyond the cliffs framed by the twin mountains. The waves were rolling in great undulating swells. Dark storm clouds churned above.

Through the office window, she saw The Man Who Held The Town Together moving in a frenzy, flipping open a box, thumbing through cards, closing the box, and moving on to the next. She hurried to the door and knocked. He thrust the door open, his eyes panicked.

"Oh, well, hello," he stammered. "You have caught me at a bad time, I . . ."

She held up the card and he immediately snatched it out of her hand, reading it over, then lunging toward her, wrapping her in a hug. His chin rested on her shoulder.

"Thankyouthankyouthankyou!" he said.

She thought of the pediatrician. It struck her how similar the first embrace and the last embrace of a relationship could be, just burning at slightly different temperatures.

He pulled away and crossed the room, closing one box, then lifting another box onto a table, opening it, carefully thumbing through cards, and sliding the renegade back into its slot.

Alexandra didn't wait to be invited in, instead stepping

inside and closing the door behind her, shutting out the now howling wind. The strange contraption ticked under the picture of the missing boy.

Wallace, Alexandra reminded herself.

She looked for a mirror to primp her tousled hair, but found none. She made do with the reflection in the window, turning just in time to catch The Man staring at her.

"Thank you," he repeated. "You have no idea the panic I was in."

"You are very welcome. Now, you must let me know your name."

The Man chuckled, his gaze passing behind her to the window. He walked around her so he could glimpse the sky.

"I am not leaving without it," Alexandra said, firmly.

"I am The Man Who Holds The Town Together," the Man said, his eyes on the clouds.

"That's not a real name."

"I know, but it's what I have." He met her eyes briefly before crossing the room to restack boxes.

"I'm not going to call you that," Alexandra said, but smiling. "We'll need to come up with something less clumsy."

The Man paused with a box in his hands as he considered.

"Jeffrey," he finally said. "No one calls me that anymore."

"Jeffrey," Alexandra said, looking at his face to see how well the name fit upon it. "Well, I'm never calling you Man, or *The* Man, and certainly not The Man Who Holds The Town Together. Jeffrey is a fine name. The others can call you what they will, but is it okay if I call you Jeffrey?"

The Man considered, a little sadly. Alexandra worried that she'd misstepped. Before she could reel back her question, he said "Yes. I suppose. You weren't here when . . . when I made the change."

"We can come up with an all-new name, if that's better. I'm always full of ideas, which you'll find out about me."

"Jeffrey is fine," The Man—Jeffrey—said. He was masking something, Alexandra realized. He wasn't ready to let her see fully within him, but a window was cracked at least.

A fat raindrop plunked against a window pane.

"The weather moves fast here," Alexandra said, watching the darkening skies.

"It does when it moves with purpose," he said.

She turned to look at him. "And what is its purpose?"

The Man gazed out across the town. "To make us slow down and sit with this moment."

Sitting with a moment

In The Town Where All Things Are Possible,

the rain fell upon the roof in thick, rhythmic sheets like an urging friend. The Man Who Held The Town Together realized he'd waited too long to kiss Alexandra while Alexandra realized she'd waited too long to kiss him.

They sat at a modest table in the dimly lit office while listening to the violence of the storm. The entire office creaked with each gust. Wallace's portrait rattled a little as it hung from the wall on a tiny nail. Alexandra was amazed that not a single drop found its way through the shuddering roof.

All along, the little machine with all the gears and unclear purposes ticked and hummed, not letting a little foul weather disturb its work.

Alexandra and The Man—Jeffrey—gazed out the window over the rooftops of brownstones towards a mountain standing before the sea, all warped and translucent through the fingers of rain tracing down the pane. She found it hard to breathe. Her eyes drew down to slight, nervous tremors shooting through Jeffrey's fingers resting inches from hers. She could not remember how long it had been since one of them had uttered a single word. The silence was intoxicating.

She thought again about the name from the card she'd found, Randall Witherspoon, and the man's wish to live one more day.

"Are you a genie?" Alexandra asked. Jeffrey only smiled. Alexandra pressed. "And is this office your magic lamp?" She gestured to the boxes. "And are all of those wishes that you are running terribly behind on fulfilling?"

Jeffrey turned from the window to face her. "Yes, you've caught me. Now I owe you three wishes, too. But as you mentioned, I'm running terribly behind."

He looked back at the rain. "I really wish I could tell you more."

"Can you tell me why you don't go by your name anymore?" Alexandra asked. "If you feel up to it."

The rain drummed down on the roof above. Thunder shook the pains.

"I failed at my job," he said, finally. "I failed and people were hurt. Died. I abandoned my name so that I could be reminded who I really am."

"I see," she said. "It's quite a burden."

"It's a privilege." The answer was quick, Alexandra noticed. Practiced. He'd had this conversation before.

"So you are only your job and nothing more?" Alexandra asked, keeping her voice soft.

They both understood the real question.

"I play darts," he said. "I try to have fun, be fun. I can be a fun guy."

"Darts are the limit of your funness?"

"I used to play golf a bit, if you'd consider that fun," Jeffrey said. "I read, if you'd consider that fun. I played a fair amount of hockey when my knees were still up to it. Though I could never skate quite as well as you."

Alexandra nodded. "It's true. I am a demon on the ice and you should be awed by my prowess."

The Man nodded in deference.

"Hockey was the last space where I felt I didn't have to

hold back," Alexandra said. "I'm an older sister. She was
... incredible. But difficult. My parents leaned on me quite
a bit."

"So you had to be a second mother?"

Alexandra took a deep breath, considering how far she
wanted to let the Man in.

"It was a privilege," she said. Tears escaped quickly and
she dried them with the back of her hand.

"I'm sorry," she said because she didn't know what else
to say.

"And she's passed?" Jeffrey asked, his voice gentle and
safe, like the creak of a church pew.

Alexandra nodded. "My family loved me, my parents
loved me, but my parents are cautious. Timid. I wished
for a life they couldn't understand. A life that would've
taken me far from home. They didn't think my sister could
survive without me nearby."

A tear escaped. "She died anyway."

Jeffrey turned in his chair to reach for a white linen
napkin. He handed it to her and Alexandra dabbed at her
eye.

"There's no good way to bring her up," Alexandra said.
"I'm still just so raw."

"I understand. And I hope you feel safe being raw
around me. For myself, I have a hard time being any other
way."

Her fingertip found embroidery on the napkin and she
glanced down at it. "J + S" had been stitched in gold, curled
serifs. She guessed it was a wedding napkin. *Jeffrey and
Sacha? Jeffrey and Sue? Jeffrey and ... Scarlette?*

"We'll make for good company," Alexandra said, flipping the napkin over discreetly. "All tears and bated breath." She sighed heavily, fortifying herself. "Is it ever possible to unbreak yourself?"

Jeffrey smirked. "Well, this is The Town Where—"

Alexandra lifted her hand, cutting him off. "Don't say it."

Jeffrey shrugged, his smile returning, warming the room like sunlight.

A drip tapped on the floor. He retrieved a ceramic bowl from a creaky cupboard, placed it on the floor, then looked up at the ceiling. "Drat." He put his palm up to catch the next drip, then reached up on his tippy toes to touch the ceiling where the drip had pushed its way through a spreading grey patch of the spackled ceiling. "Well, nothing to do about it right now."

He turned to Alexandra. "What life did you wish for when you were a child wanting to go far, far away?"

"To cross the sea," she said. "To live a thousand lives. To take too many risks, to fail too many times, to succeed at something grand at least once. God, I sound like a terrible pop song."

"I like terrible pop songs," Jeffrey said. "I could stand to have one more in my life."

Alexandra dabbed at more tears. "Same."

Jeffrey stretched and looked back out the window, assessing the storm.

"Well, this is a small town," he said. "Options for adventure are limited." He leaned against the small kitchenette counter. "But there are some risks to be had."

"Darts, for instance," Alexandra said. "Especially if they are steel-tipped. They could do some damage."

"You're kidding, but I could snipe a swallow at twenty paces."

Alexandra smirked at that, tapping her fingers on the tabletop. "I'm sure we could find something a bit more exciting than darts, though." She met his eyes. "If we put our heads together."

"Maybe. I'm also a little out of practice—on things fun and exciting. I've been alone for a long time."

"That must be hard," Alexandra said.

"It is. But I try to remind myself that, well . . ."

"You're still alive?"

"Oh, it sounds so awful to hear it out loud," he said. "We're both just terrible pop songs, aren't we? But yes. I'm still alive and she would want me to remember that. My wife, I mean."

"What was her name?" Alexandra asked.

"Samantha."

"Samantha," Alexandra said, softly, committing it to memory. "Is it okay to talk about her?"

Jeffrey chuckled. "I should ask you the same." He picked at a groove in the counter's finish. "I am fine talking about her if you want to know, but I think that should be another time." He looked up at her. "Don't you?"

Alexandra nodded. The moment felt right. Yet neither moved.

"So you own a bookstore now?" Jeffrey said. "How's that going?"

"Swimmingly. I've been open less than one day and

already abandoned my store to two elderly strangers so I can hang out with a man who wouldn't tell me his first name until our second date."

"Our second date? You're very generous to consider this"—he gestured around his meager office with a leaking roof—"a date."

Alexandra arched an eyebrow. "It's not the setting that makes a date, it's the company."

Jeffrey smiled like a clumsy schoolboy.

"Anyway," she said. "I guess my new life plan is to read books in my little shop until I'm crushed by an avalanche of dusty paperbacks. I'm eager to become the most boring person in the entire town."

"I don't believe you," Jeffrey said. "I think this is just a cover until you've devised a brilliant plot to seize control of our harbor for some nefarious reason."

Alexandra lifted an eyebrow and gave the subtlest of nods. "I'll never tell." She rose from the table and walked to the window that looked out toward the twin mountains and the sea. "But perhaps you should try to root it out of me along with all my other secrets. In the best interest of the town."

He joined her at the window. "I aim to."

Her heart thrummed. *Just kiss me already!* she wanted to scream.

"I'm glad you're here," he said instead. "That bookstore is important to this town. It gives us a taste of what's beyond. We're a little isolated, as I'm sure you've noticed."

"I have," Alexandra said. "I just hope there are enough readers in the town to support me and my devious plot to carve out my section of the sea."

"Is that your first wish?" he asked.

Alexandra tilted her head as she considered the question. "I mean, you can write it down on the card, but if I get to prioritize, I have other things more front of mind."

"Such as?"

Alexandra blushed deeply, sweat reaching her pores. She now yearned for the silence to return.

"Oh, I mean—um, from The Town," Jeffrey stammered. "From The Town Where, well, All Things Are, um, you know."

Alexandra chuckled, no less nervous, but thankful for the escape. She pulled her hand in closer, retreating it from the playing field. He folded his arms. He had waited too long to kiss her and she'd waited too long to kiss him. It would need to happen another time.

She took a deep breath, feeling the tension clearing at last, the fog dissipating, her mind regaining clarity. She thought. She thought. She thought. She remembered.

"I would wish for a second chance at saving someone," she finally said. "Is that possible? Ever possible? Even here? To save someone."

The Man Who Held The Town Together didn't answer, but the storm, showing some empathy, cleared from the sky. The rain ceased abruptly. Almost comically. Alexandra looked at the sky to find the sun peeking from the clouds, about to set.

"Oh, shoot, what time is it?" she asked. "I have to get back to my shop!"

"I'm sure it's fine, but may I walk you to it?"

"Sure," she said with a generous smile.

He led her to the door. Opening it for her, he placed his hand delicately on the small of her back for just a moment as she passed, the brief touch sparking a shiver that shimmied up her spine. She laughed, strode across the sidewalk, and stomped two-footed into a puddle. The splash haloed out away from her, nearly reaching Jeffrey's shoes. Alexandra spun to face him, her eyebrow arched.

"I like puddles," she said, seriously.

"I see that."

"It's important for you to accept that or this entire thing is doomed," she said.

"Yes, ma'am."

She saw him hold a breath, his eyes widening. He wanted to act, yet hesitating.

Be strong, she called to him in her mind.

He stepped toward her, extended his hand. She laced her fingers with his.

Close enough.

They began walking. At some point, they reached the bottom of the hill. At some point, they passed downtown, then they reached Wider World of Books and Novelties. It was dark; the door was locked. Reeves and Róisín had done her a good turn.

At some point Alexandra and Jeffrey walked on and entered the countryside. Time had been a fluid thing from the moment they clasped hands. They could've been walking for minutes or hours or days.

The rain returned and trapped them under the tin roof of an aged bus stop. A crooked streetlight bathed the small shelter in yellow light, the only light along the lonely road. The rain pounded above. Their hands had yet to unlatch, even as she wiped the rain from her face and laughed. She glanced around the small shelter.

"Why is there a bus stop way out here?" she asked.

"Because we needed one," he answered.

"The town?"

"No. Just you and I."

He lifted his free hand to her face to clear away raindrops. She rested her cheek on his palm. A breath of time passed. They fell together, their lips meeting first. Their hands unlaced, finally free to explore.

Hold on to this! she pleaded with herself. *Hold on to it. Hold on.*

In The Town Where All Things Are Possible,

Alexandra and The Man Who Held The Town Together parted ways at the shop's threshold as the rising sun glowed across the rooftops. She couldn't understand how an entire night had passed while they kissed, walked, kissed, walked. Her feet ached.

As she watched him go, Roison's voice rose above the morning bird call: "It's happened, Reeves! Two days, just like I said!"

The Man—Jeffrey—hurried his walk and Alexandra retreated into her store.

But I will see him again, she thought as she leaned against the door. *I will make space for him and he will make space for me. The Town will provide.*

She considered sleeping a few hours before opening the shop, but instead she opened the door back up to the town and whatever it brought her today. She plucked a sheet of paper from a notepad and wrote:

> *Alexandra Forrest*
> *I wish for time and the wisdom to recognize its true value.*

She folded it two times, then tucked it inside the register, beneath the coin tray until she figured out what Jeffrey did with his notecards.

On the register was a little note:

> *Dinner is in the fridge,*
> *—Mr. and Mrs. Reeves*

Her stomach awoke, so she crossed through the store and scaled the spiral staircase to reach the loft. She thought of how everyone talked about the Wider World Books & Novelties—a monument representing an idea the townspeople liked, and thought worthy of support. She worried that each person assumed that the support would come from someone else.

How often had she been thrilled to find a theatre, but never attended a play; discovered a record store, but never purchased a record player; and stepped into a bookstore, but never finding the time to read?

"If Aunt Tabitha made it work, I can, too."

She hurried towards a small, cramped kitchenette tucked into what was once a projection booth. A sink, cabinets, and microwave on one side faced a small stovetop and fridge on the other. A dark window looked out into the theatre where she could barely make out rows of wooden chairs and a stage. She walked through the kitchenette to a door she assumed would be a pantry, but was in fact the tiniest bathroom she'd ever seen, with a narrow shower and a toilet tucked under a medicine cabinet. No sink. The kitchen would have to do.

"Well," Alexandra said, then sighed. She tested the shower. After a couple minutes, the hot water finally arrived. "Could be worse."

She closed the restroom and opened the fridge door, which barely had the room to open fully without banging into the stove. She realized the only way to get into the fridge was to enter the bathroom first, which she did so she could retrieve a casserole dish with a virgin shepherd's pie with dollops of mashed potatoes like untouched ski hills. Her stomach urged her to hurry.

She spooned out a hearty ration onto a plate, then popped it in the microwave. As her meal heated up, she steeped in the savory aroma filling the kitchenette. She leaned over the small sink towards a window looking down to the theatre. She cupped her hand over her eyes, but it was far too dark to make out more than just shadows of long unused seats.

Carrying a heaping plate and a glass of water, she circled down the spiral staircase as it groaned in protest.

And there, at the counter, stood the woman in the clockwork mask—Tessa.

"Hello!" Alexandra called while trying not to spill her shepherd's pie.

Tessa turned her head enough to bring around her one exposed eye. She gave Alexandra a broad, practiced smile as Alexandra approached.

Alexandra tried, and failed, to not stare at the contraption which was affixed to the right side of Tessa's face with an ornately stamped leather strap. The tiny gears ticked delicately, moving in rhythm, like veins pulsing with a heartbeat. Alexandra couldn't guess at the contraption's function.

"Good morning," Alexandra said, setting her plate and water on a shelf beneath the counter.

"I'm unreasonably excited to help you rearrange this store," Tessa said. "Do you mind?" Tessa didn't wait for permission. She plunged into the nearest aisle, her purple satin gown rustling with each movement. "I've no idea how your aunt could live in this chaos."

"You haven't even seen under the counter yet," Alexandra said. "I love your dress, by the way. You always look so exquisite."

"Thank you, dear," Tessa answered as she brushed her fingertips along the spines of books, turning her attention from one side of the aisle to the other.

"Should I be following you, or . . . ?"

Tessa's dress continued rustling as she disappeared into the labyrinth. "No, let me reacquaint myself, then we'll talk."

Alexandra turned to the register. "Oh. Okay, I probably need to focus on learning how this stupid thing works so I can actually record sales."

"I'll show you later," Tessa said from within the stacks. "I used to work for Tabitha in the summers when I was younger. I can shed some light."

"Was that when she did all her traveling, in the summers?" Alexandra asked.

"Tabitha? No. Never. She loved the shop and only hired kids to give them something to do when school was out."

Alexandra couldn't square the memory of her aunt as a brazen adventurer with that of a quiet shopkeeper dutifully minding the register day after day after day. She gazed across the shop, the shelves a riot of colorful spines, the loft overlooking everything.

The doorbell rang as the door cracked open. Wendy walked in with a satchel. Her ring of keys jingled at her hip while she walked.

"Oh, you're here, too!" Alexandra said.

"I am," Wendy said, hoisting the heavy satchel onto the counter. She unzipped it and retrieved a leatherbound journal. "Ready to work."

"Hello, Wendy," Tessa called from within the stacks.

"Tessa!" Wendy said, delighted, then looked at Alexandra. "You're in good hands."

Wendy walked into the labyrinth, journal in hand, pen clicking. Soon Alexandra could hear hushed whispers passing between the two women, scheming with no apparent interest in including Alexandra.

The doorbell chimed again and Alexndra turned to see Gerald, a heavy grocery sack in one arm and his portfolio in the other.

"Morning," he called.

Alexandra glanced at the stacks to see if Tessa was in view—she wasn't—then burned back to Gerald whose curious eyebrows now tilted inwards.

"Oh hi, Gerald," Alexandra said at the exact volume needed to instruct multiple people that an awkward moment had arrived.

"Yeah, hi," Gerald said, then smiled with his wild supernova of a mustache.

Tessa's dress rustled as she approached. "Hello, Gerald."

Gerald dipped his eyes away to an empty magazine rack by the counter as his mustache twitched. "Oh, hi, Tessa." Wendy came up behind Tessa. "Wendy," Gerald added, then looked at Alexandra. "Alexandra."

With everyone now accounted for, Gerald sat the grocery sack on the counter. "Your breakfast," he said, then turned to quickly slip back out the door.

"Ladies, I'll be right back," Alexandra said.

They nodded.

Alexandra hurried around the counter and out the front door.

"Gerald," she called and he paused his frantic scurry just as he reached the street corner. He looked both ways for traffic, as if he was considering the odds of a successful escape from Alexandra, his pursuer. He finally turned slowly around, eyes down like a penitent puppy.

"Thank you for the breakfast, but a deal's a deal," Alexandra said, snapping her fingers and holding out her right hand for him to deliver his portfolio. Gerald sulked back towards the shop, glancing in the window briefly, then back to the sidewalk in front of him.

"Stop making it more awkward than it has to be," Alexandra said. "Show me what you've got."

Gerald still hesitated, gathering courage. Alexandra snapped her fingers again. He handed over the portfolio. Alexandra sat down on the window ledge and patted the space next to her.

As she unzipped the portfolio, she said, "Look, girls hate this wounded puppy act. I get it, I'm sorry you're heartbroken, but try to relax and it'll be way easier for both of you to co-exist in this tiny town again."

Perhaps she thought a little of The Man Who Held the Town Together as she said it.

"I know, I know," Gerald said. "Father says the same thing. 'Gerald, you worry too much. Gerald, you feel too much.' And this from a man who loves Morrissey more than his own family. It's just, I don't know. I never know how to make my face look normal."

"Ha, I've been there," Alexandra said, then turned her attention to the portfolio.

Within was a pencil sketch of the bookshop, perfect perspective, graphite shadows, a little note he'd made to himself: "Watercolor?" On the marquee, "Welcome home, Alexandra!"

"Oh my," she said, running her fingers over the paper ever so lightly. She looked at Gerald and smiled. "Thank you. And yes, definitely watercolor."

He nodded, a bashful smile peaking through his mustache.

Alexandra turned the page to find a two-story, narrow, cylindrical brick tower with a metal door. It looked like a bunker had sprouted out of the ground. A grassy field surrounded it, trees in the distance, then the mountains and the ocean beyond.

"What's this?" she asked.

"The library!" Gerald said. "It's on the south side of the town, a bit out of the way."

Alexandra looked back down at the portfolio. "How is this a library? It's so tiny."

"It's mostly underground, and it's not really a book-type library," Gerald said. "It's difficult to explain, but it's . . . library. You'll just need to see it for yourself."

"A library without any books," Alexandra said. "Yes, I'll need to see it for myself."

Alexandra flipped to the third and last sketch. It was a tavern with a simple hand-carved sign that read, a bit too on the nose, "The Tavern Where All Things Are Possible."

Alexandra chuckled. "Of course. I think I saw this at the base of the hill, close to the town circle by . . . oh, what was it Wendy called the sewer?"

"God's Blowhole," Gerald said. "And yes, just around the corner."

Alexandra flipped back to the sketch of her store. "Yes, watercolor. If you finish it and I can ever afford it, I'd love to buy this from you." She zipped back up the portfolio and handed it to the nervous young man. "Thank you for showing me the town. I'd love to see more, when you have time."

"I'll make time." Gerald stood, nodded, turned away, turned back, glanced in the shop. "And I'll try to be less weird."

"Yes, please do," Alexandra said. "Practice your face in the mirror. If you encounter Tessa, ask general, breezy questions. Let her believe that you can be just friends, and the walls will tumble down." Alexandra stood. "Or maybe they won't, but at least you will have tried. We love who we love for a reason. It's a shame to let such a temporal thing as heartbreak destroy a perfectly good friendship."

Gerald smiled wider, bolder, his supernova mustache almost tickling his nose. He nodded, then scurried towards the grocery store.

Alexandra returned to her shop, finding Tessa and Wendy at the front counter looking over notes in Wendy's journal. Tessa looked up, her one exposed eye looking out the window, then to Alexandra. "He really is a sweet man. When my accident happened . . . " She touched her mask. "I should've died. Mr. Witherspoon made this for me. He was our town tinkerer and it did the trick. But it was hard, and recovery was long. Through it all, Gerald stayed with me and he did his best to keep my spirits up."

"But?" Alexandra asked.

"He's too much," Tessa said. "As friends, we were perfect. Inseparable. As lovers . . . " She sighed as the gears ticked. "I wish he would find someone new, someone who can make him happy."

"He can and he will," Alexandra said. "It is the Town Where All Things Are Possible, right?"

Tessa smiled. "That's mostly just a clever name."

"Well," Alexandra said. "That's disappointing because I had some grand aspirations of lion taming and soothsaying."

Tessa looked at Alexandra with her one exposed eye. "The lions would eat our penguins."

"Oh, right," Alexandra said. With some effort to pull the conversation to less fraught ground, she added, "any thoughts on how to bring sanity to this bookstore?"

Wendy clapped her journal closed. "Not yet," she said. "We have some questions for you."

Alexandra braced herself. "Okay?"

Wendy sat the journal down on the counter, approached Alexandra, and held out a hand. After a brief hesitation, Alexandra accepted. Wendy held her other hand out to Tessa, who joined them. They stood like conspiring children, like a circle of spinsters, like . . .

"Are we a coven now?" Alexandra asked, hoping the answer was yes. She gasped. "A bookshop coven!"

Tessa tilted her head, considering.

"Focus," Wendy said, pressing on. "Close your eyes."

"I've always wanted to join a coven," Alexandra whispered.

"Focus," Wendy said. "This shop was once Tabitha's, but she passed it to you. Not as a steward, but as its new guiding force. We are not here to fit you within the shop, but to fit the shop within you. Imagine how you can extend your being into this space, and from there, we will know how to remake the Wider World into a reflection of you."

"But I didn't choose any of these books," Alexandra said, eyes still closed. "The books are the store, and these books are Tabitha."

"Shh," whispered Wendy. "The books are passengers. They come, they go. With each book sold, Tabitha makes more space for you."

Alexandra understood, but also thought of how long it would take to cycle through a store stuffed from wall to wall with Tabitha. "I feel like a usurper."

"You are a savior," Tessa said, squeezing Alexandra's hand. "Now imagine."

Alexandra focused, picturing the books sweeping off the shelves until the shop was bare. Then the shelves themselves faded. Then the counter and all their clutter, leaving an empty lobby.

Who am I? Alexandra thought. And how can I fit this shop within me?

"I want to travel to every nation on the globe," Alexandra said aloud, still imagining the empty store. "I want to travel to every planet, to every galaxy. I want to live every adventure."

"So that's how we arrange the store," Wendy said.

"Adventure by adventure," Tessa added.

In Alexandra's mind, the bookshop was still empty. She sighed. "I still can't see it."

"You will," Wendy said, releasing Alexandra's hand, then Tessa released too.

Alexandra peeked to find her fellow bookshop witches watching her.

"We need to do a cleansing," Wendy said. "And I have an idea. We will reconvene the bookshop coven later this week."

Wendy winked at Alexandra, stuffed her journal into the satchel, and waved on her way out the door.

Alexandra hurried after. "Oh, I want to come see the library."

"And you will," Wendy called back. "But not until we've remade the Wider World."

Alexandra turned to Tessa, whose one serious eye aimed back.

"You want to see the world?" Tessa asked.

"Yes. I've always wanted to . . . get in a boat and just aim at a star. Haven't you?"

Tessa's frown deepened. "The Man Who Holds The Town Together won't leave. No matter what you do. He is anchored here. Irreprebably."

"I see," Alexandra said, anger stirring. She knew Tessa was right, of course, but it could've remained unspoken.

Tessa took Alexandra's hands in both of hers. "I am happy for you. For this store, for this new life you can have here, but I also won't lie to you. We seem a happy, simple town, but there is so much wreckage. The Man is kind, but he is more troubled than all of us. He's been battered and tossed by life. Even if his work hadn't chained him to that little office on the hill, I don't believe he'd have the strength to leave. Be careful or you'll get chained, too."

Then Tessa swept out the door in her Victorian dress, the allure of a bookshop coven leaving with her.

In The Town Where All Things Are Possible,

the Man Who Held The Town Together had spoken only once about his mysterious job of sorting thousands of cards every day. All the town's residents were, of course, curious about what happened in that little office on the hill, but generation after generation after generation chose to leave it a mystery rather than spoiling a good thing.

The Man cradled his whiskey glass that sad night as he revealed more about his job than any other Man who'd come before. "You see, it's imbalance that makes everything work here."

He was still dressed in a simple black suit with a pink rose pinned to his jacket, a memento from his wife's funeral earlier that day.

"In the world outside, the predators will always have the edge. Always. They consume, consume, consume. Society will always reward them; Darwin assured us of that. But here, we can disrupt the laws of nature. We can lure the predators away, leaving the rest of us to simple and happy lives."

"What does that have to do with sorting cards all day?" asked The Man's best friend. Leo maintained a five-hole golf course to the south of town, at the base of one of the twin mountains. It was a hilly, weed-ridden tangle of doglegs and unintended water hazards, but it satisfied Leo and the rest of the town's golf enthusiasts. Due to a lack of investment, the "greens" were just carefully leveled sand traps. Back then, The Man played golf with Leo every Friday night, rushing through the five-hole course as the sun settled into the horizon.

"I just don't see how it's all related," Leo said. The Man downed the last of his whiskey and slid the glass toward the bartender, Dajuan, a tall, dark-skinned man with a distinguished grey-and-black beard. Dajaun had retired from textile imports to take over The Tavern Where All Things Are Possible. He hated the name of his tavern, but understood that the tourists needed something to giggle about.

The Man called for another whiskey, and Dajuan obliged. "All things are possible," the Man said, then took a sip. He flinched from the burn. "All things are possible, but not all things are advisable."

The Man had survived the funeral only by not uttering a word to anyone. He couldn't be touched, he couldn't be consoled. He was a fragile thing of ice and cracks.

But it was Friday, so Leo forced him outside for a quick round of golf. The Man played in his dress shoes and never removed his jacket. Neither man spoke. The only sounds were the crunch of dry grass, the ping of clubs striking balls, and the distant call of sea birds.

Next came the tavern and a game of darts. The Man's hands were shaky and inelegant. Leo did his best not to win, but the game needed to be won by someone. After the drinks finally took hold, The Man opened up more than he had since taking over the lonely office on the top of the hill.

"You can't blame yourself for this," Dajuan told The Man. "Even this town isn't immune to the horrible things that humans do."

"We are immune," the Man said, tipping back the rest of the whiskey. "I work, we live, we prosper. I don't work, the world's evils claw their way in."

"Jeffrey—" Leo said, putting his hand on his friend's shoulder.

"Don't call me that,"The Man said, jerking away. "Never again."

And that was the last The Man spoke of it, tipping his glass over and splashing whiskey across the bar. He staggered out of the tavern and, effectively, out of Leo's life. It would be days before anyone saw The Man emerge again from the office, and when he did, The Man was never the same.

"I want him back," Leo told Alexandra as he recounted the story at the very same bartop. She'd walked into the town's only tavern after waiting all day for Jeffrey to show up at the Wider World. Her pride wouldn't allow her to seek him out at his office again, but she guessed that he would likely pass by the bar on his way home from his office for a round of darts. She positioned herself on a stool in the middle of the bartop, which would be easily seen to anyone passing by the large window facing the hill. She wanted to at least pretend to be a little coy.

Leo recognized her immediately, as the town spread intel fast. Leo, in turn, sat down on the stool next to her to dole out intel on The Man Who Held The Town Together.

"None of us understand The Man Who Holds The Town Together," Leo grunted, then tipped back the mug to finish his beer. He swept the foam from his bushy blond beard. "But for as long as this town has been what it is, there has been someone in that office, sorting cards into boxes, quietly going mad."

"Jeffrey doesn't seem crazy to me," Alexandra said.

Leo grinned down at her.

"He told you his old name, did he?"

"I'm persuasive," she said with a proud tilt to her chin.

"He's not crazy, you're right," Dajuan said, pulling the tap to fill another mug with beer. "I've known crazy men. Many crazy men. He is in pain and all alone." Dajuan slid the beer across the bartop. "Or rather, he was alone." Dajuan winked at Alexandra and she blushed just a bit.

"Well, The Man has always been with us," Leo said. "But also apart from us. Something about what he has to do builds a wall around him that none of us can get through. We worry, but we won't defy tradition."

"Defy?" Alexandra asked.

"Get between him and his job," Leo said, bringing the new frothy mug to his lips.

"So I should stay out of his way?" Alexandra asked with a touch of anger.

"No, God no," Leo said, giving her a sly smile. "He's a good man. He works too much, and that might never change. But he is worthy of you, no doubt in my mind. You'd be doing all of us a favor by stepping right in between him and that damned job of his. Come what may."

Alexandra looked at Dajuan and asked, "Come what may?"

Dajuan shrugged. "At least I'll finally be able to rename this bar to something less embarrassing."

Alexandra grinned and lifted her mug. "Thank you."

A soccer match played silently on a small television hanging above the bar. They watched a forward flail to the ground, holding his ankle, while a referee shook his head "no" and motioned for the player to stand back up.

The trio grunted disapprovingly, almost in harmony.

"And his wife was murdered?" Alexandra asked. She'd held the question in too long already. "Any idea who did it?"

"He believes it was the town's punishment," Leo said. "He might be right. He might be wrong. She is dead either way."

A player broke from a mess of legs and cleats, dribbling the ball up the field at a frenzied sprint. He planted, he kicked, but the goalie leapt like a cat to punch the ball up over the goal.

"Damn," Dajuan said. He turned and gestured to Alexandra's glass. She shook her head no.

"It destroyed him," Leo said, looking away from the television. "Tore him up. Still does. He smiles when I see him, we shake hands, but he's not there anymore. No, his mind is always in that office. Trapped there, his body just allowed to wander out in the daylight from time to time."

"I saw you two at the ice rink," Dajuan said. "He's not trapped when he's with you."

Leo chuckled. "Yeah, I heard about that. He's better. He's the old Jeff—"

Leo clipped off the name just in time, exchanging a glance with the Dajuan.

"Goddamn superstitions," Leo said, shaking his head and taking another drink. "May they all fall down that miserable sewer grate so that we can have our friend back."

"Hear, hear," Dajuan said.

Alexandra considered the soccer match, she considered the office on the hill, she considered the ocean beyond and all the adventures to be found.

She considered love, then its weight and whether it was worth bearing.

Finally she considered Jeffrey, and it was like the sun finally broke through the clouds.

"I have to go to him," Alexandra said. "He won't come to me. Right?"

"Right," Leo said. "I'm sorry to say that there is no easy path to him or with him."

"Well, not tonight," Alexandra said. "I can make him wait another day. For dignity's sake."

"I hope I haven't scared you off him," Leo said. "He's a good man. The best of us, really. He's just ensnared in something far bigger than all of us."

"A hell of a thing," Dajuan said, then looked at Alexandra. "But at least you know what you're getting yourself into."

In The Town Where All Things Are Possible,

The Man didn't come to the bar. He didn't tap at the window of the bookshop later in the night, he didn't slip a note through the door or serenade her from the street. Alexandra slept fretfully in the ancient, squeaky bed on a mattress still shaped to her aunt. She rose to the smell of dusty books and rain dripping onto the flat roof above her.

In the kitchenette, as the water dripped through the coffee grounds of the pour-over filter, she gazed into the darkness of the theatre.

She would look for the key again today.

She took her mug and stood at the railing overlooking the shop. She closed her eyes and imagined how to fit the shop within. Who was she? What about her was big enough, yet simple enough to be the idea, the force that drove the shop?

Her eyes snapped open. She pulled her luggage out from under her bed and dug through spare clothes, a porcelain cat wrapped in a tube sock, and other novelties from her life before. She moved one case off another, then opened it. Rummaging through shirts rolled up over delicate trinkets and paperbacks from her childhood, she finally found her well-worn world atlas. Its cover was torn and stained with her nine-year-old fingerprints, the map was outdated and included nations that had fractured and fallen decades prior, but it would do. She opened the atlas to a double-page spread of the entire planet in faded greens and reds and blues.

She carried it to the balcony and held it over the store.

That was how the store would fit, she thought.

Eager to talk to her bookshop coven, she tossed on clothes and hustled down the groaning circular staircase. She opened the door, ready to race through the streets with her brilliant idea, but was stilled by music.

The distant, pained wail of a brass band echoed throughout the town. She also heard a howling tenor singing in a language she didn't understand. Or perhaps it wasn't a language at all, but simply the sound of sorrow. She tucked the atlas under her arm, closed and locked the door, and walked towards the music.

Lights were off at every brownstone, no children playing, no grandchildren shuffling after. Baskets of pink roses decorated each stoop. She turned corner after corner, chasing the music echoing off the buildings. The music was moving, she realized. She hurried, winding down a row of houses with lush English gardens.

Then she found them. All of the townspeople.

Billy and his march of penguins trotted ahead of the brass band, decked out in golden frills and tall, exquisite hats. A somber parade of citizens followed, all dressed in black, including a child dressed as an astronaut who'd spraypainted his costume. With him was everyone she'd met thus far and hundreds more. She spotted Dajuan the bartender, who wore an exquisite pin-striped suit and the man in his bowler who'd howled poetry up at a storm.

A dead man she'd never met laid on top of a simple wooden plank held aloft by pallbearers. The dead man held something small and metallic to his chest. His open eyes gazed lifelessly at the midday sun. He appeared to be no more than sixty, yet she could see from his gaunt face and veined hands that a sickness had wasted the man early, eating the life from him day by day until death arrived as a savior.

"Hello Mr. Witherspoon," Alexandria whispered, remembering the note she'd delivered back to The Man. "I hope your genie found your wish in time."

The Man Who Held The Town Together was one of the six pallbearers. He saw her, then nodded with a tight smile. Enough to show he was glad to see her, but now was not the time. She understood and her heart warmed.

Walking ahead of the pallbearers was Gabriel Gratherson, the painter and son of the woman who'd brought Alexandra and Jeffrey fried pies on their first date. Gabriel's bright blue eyes aimed at the sky as he sang a perfect, heart-breaking song in Portuguese. His beard glistened in the morning sun. His voice both led and followed the brass band in a way only made possible by years of practice, years of funeral marches, years of sorrow.

Alexandria didn't dwell on the spectacle, instead accepted it as she understood she would need to accept all the strange happenings of the town.

Alexandra spotted Wendy and Tessa, who was pushing Mrs. Gratherson in a wheelchair. Alexandra slipped into the crowd beside them.

Mrs. Gratherson reached out and took Alexandra's hand in hers. They smiled at each other warmly, then walked on as the penguins led the march through the town and on toward the cliffs looking out over the sea. They aimed for the valley directly between the towering twin mountains, a brief space for the sheltered town to glimpse the wider world.

The clouds were rolling in like a thin grey blanket the town was pulling over itself for comfort. The march stopped twenty feet from the cliffs, where a path opened to allow the pallbearers to pass with the body. A young woman in a fedora and a black three-piece suit followed the pallbearers, her head down, a pink rose in her hands.

The pallbearers lowered the body from their shoulders and held the dead man at waist level. The young woman walked to the man, ran her hand over his cheek, then opened his mouth. She plucked the stem from the pink rose and placed the blossom in his mouth.

Clouds eclipsed the sun. The young woman kissed the man on his forehead. She lifted his hands, placing them down onto the plank so she could retrieve the metal contraption resting on his chest. She stepped back from the body. The pallbearers looked at one another. The Man nodded.

They lifted the plank up on their shoulders again, stepped toward the cliff. Gabriel's voice, accompanied by the swelling notes of the band, rose to a soaring crescendo. Then the song faded and Gabriel retreated amid the rest of the procession. The pallbearers tipped the plank. Mr. Witherspoon slid off and plummeted to the waves below.

Alexandria gasped. Mrs. Gratherson's grip tightened on her hand.

"It's what he wanted," Mrs. Gratherson whispered. "It's our way."

Rain fell, but only along the cliff and over the sea, as if

to throw a curtain over the dead man as the waves carried him out into the ocean.

Not a single drop reached the funeral procession.

With no regard for the weather phenomenon, the procession turned and marched back toward the town. The pallbearers fell in with the rest of the town's residents. Only the young woman watched the sea, left alone with her loss.

"Who was he?" Alexandria whispered to Mrs. Gratherson.

"A tinkerer," Mrs. Gratherson said. "He was sick for a very long time. He was holding out for his daughter to return from Chicago. She arrived yesterday. He died very early this morning."

So his genie didn't fail him after all, Alexandra thought.

"I found one of Jeffrey's cards," she said. "He'd lost it somehow. The card had 'Randall Witherspoon' on it. He was asking to l—."

Mrs. Gratherson yanked Alexandria close as her eyes grew hard.

"Don't!" Mrs. Gratherson said, then released Alexandra's hand. Tessa frowned, then whispered into Mrs. Gratherson's ear. Tessa turned to show her one exposed eye to Alexandra, giving the slightest of nods, then pushed the old woman along with the procession.

Alexandria stood still, confused and ashamed, as the parade passed by her. She still had the atlas with her, the brilliant idea still on the vine.

Then the brass band struck up a jubilant jazz melody. The townspeople loosened, many danced, many sang, the clouds broke, the sun found the town again. A funeral ended, a celebration began.

Alexandra turned to the daughter still standing at the cliff's edge. She thought about going to her, but Alexandra had misstepped once already. The woman walked to the cliff's edge, then placed the contraption on the ground. She wound a lever on it several times, then stood back. The contraption unfurled, spreading out wings, and rose into the air. With a flap of its wings, the metal bird launched into the air and flew out over the water. Alexandra gasped at the sight of the strange, gleaming bird soaring up into the sky above the ocean.

Then, its momentum exhausted, the tiny metal bird plunged down into the waves.

Alexandra felt a twinge of shame, as if she'd intruded on a private moment, so she turned and hurried to rejoin the procession-turned-parade.

As they flooded back into town, residents hurried into houses, emerging shortly thereafter wearing bright, elaborate costumes of smirking crows, bulbous stars, and hungry wolves. Other residents brought out instruments—violins, trumpets, guitars, hand drums, anything that could be carried, anything that could be played. While the musicians filled the town with song, the rest of the town danced and drank and told stories of the deceased Mr. Witherspoon. He was a funny man, Alexandra learned, he loved a drink, he loved his land, he loved a prank. One man bemoaned being handcuffed to a forty-pound iron weight the moment he stepped out of the church with his new bride. Another recalled waking one morning to find his car completely disassembled in his front yard.

He'd fixed grandfather clocks, bicycles, watches, buses, and anything else mechanical. He taught at the school, he volunteered at the health clinic, he was beloved and Alexandra wished she'd had the chance to know him.

"A more aggravating and charming man you'll never meet," Connor Reeves told Alexandra. "Oh, the misery and joy he'd caused you."

Music rang through the town, no longer led by Gabriel's voice; pockets of songs crashed into one another as the entire town converged near God's Blowhole. Alexandria walked to the edge of the square, keeping close to the shadows. A feast was laid out on tables lining the square, circling the mysterious stormdrain. Streamers hung from storefronts, blowing in the wind. The Greek grocer held a tray of finger food while passing through the crowd and singing "Girlfriend in a Coma."

Also standing apart from the crowd was Jeffrey. He held a beer but didn't drink it.

Alexandra wanted to flee to the Wider World, to hide within the stories of distant lands and simple romances. She wanted to begin remaking the store in her own image. But she also wanted to be near Jeffrey. Her heart was twisted and contorted and uncertain. She waited for fate to nudge her in one direction or another.

"So, you're the one?" a voice said behind her.

Alexandra turned to see the daughter of Mr. Witherspoon, the brim of her Fedora molded like a gentle wave crossing just above her face. Her lips were painted the black of her suit, her eye shadow on the verge of theatrical. There was poise in the way she lifted her chin, something learned, something that exuded wealth and status.

The town was too small for her, Alexandra thought.

"You're who Jeffrey is going to abandon his post for," the woman said.

"I . . . ," Alexandra stammered. "I'm sorry for your loss."

The woman nodded, eyes passing from Alexandra to the townspeople singing and joking.

"I can't stand it here," the woman said.

"Why?" Alexandra asked, her voice gentle, trying to exude safety.

The woman took a sharp breath and dabbed at an escaping tear with a black satin pocket square. A slight smudge of eyeliner blotted on her skin. The woman dabbed again. The smudge was gone.

"It's so suffocating," the woman said, then nodded outward, away from the town. "It's so small. They have no idea what the real world is like."

The woman shook her head, pulled off her fedora, and ran her fingers through her blonde hair.

"I don't have time for this," she said, then walked from the town square. Alexandra knew she'd never see the woman again.

Alexandra walked to the Man. He met her eyes, straightened a bit.

"You did it," Alexandra said. "One more day."

Jeffrey nodded. "Not me, the town."

"But how?"

Jeffrey shrugged, though of course he knew. He drank his beer as an excuse not to answer.

"Hey," Alexandra said, finally opening the atlas. "I've got

an idea for the store. What to do with it. Tessa and Wendy came by yesterday and we chatted."

She opened up the atlas to show the double-page spread of Earth. "It's called the Wider World, so it needs to look like the wider world. To walk into the store is to set sail for adventures both near and far."

Jeffrey considered the idea. "I love it. I love it so much." He looked at Alexandra. "What can I do to help?"

Alexandra laughed. "No idea. There are books everywhere in that store, so there's no room to work until I sell them, but how can I sell them if I have no idea what any of them are or what they're about?"

"You need a fresh canvas," Jeffrey said.

"Exactly what Tessa and Wendy said. But I'm not sure how to do that any other way than blatant arson."

Jeffrey nodded. "I know a better way. Do you have plans tomorrow?"

Alexandra shook her head, delighted at the intrigue.

"Good," he said. "It's going to be a long day, then we'll have dinner to celebrate."

"Celebrate what?"

Jeffrey backed away from her, a glint in his eyes. "A blank canvas."

Then he strolled through the crowd, motioning at Wendy, Tessa, and a few others Alexandra had yet to meet. Even Billy the penguin joined the huddle, and it was clear that a scheme was about to be launched.

How to clear a canvas

In The Town Where All Things Are Possible,

not a single soul entered the Wider World of Books and Novelties. In the lonely hours from when she returned from the funeral until closing time, Alexandra:

- Ate a delicious bowl of yogurt, granola, and fresh fruit
- Cleared out the shelves behind the register, discarding all but unused notepads and the box of customer cards
- Unpacked her clothes into a modest chest of drawers and pinned up postcards of places she'd never been, like:
  - The Canals of Venice
  - The desert mountains of Turkmenistan
  - The weekend markets of Bangkok
- Ate a fragrant quinoa, olive, tomato, and feta salad for a late lunch when she finally remembered to eat

All the while, she poked her head over the railing down into the shop which was, as she suspected, still empty.

I'll never sell another book ever again.

She brought her salad bowl back to the kitchenette to wash it, then spared a glance through the projection window leading to the darkened theatre. On a hunch, she hunted for a flashlight by throwing open every drawer in the kitchen, finally finding a heavy marine flashlight with a wide lamphead and a hard rubber handle. She clicked it on, but nothing happened. She slapped it. It startled awake and shot out a blinding yellow light.

"Wow!" Alexandra said, blinking away the red burn in her eyes.

She flipped a metal latch on the old window and, with some effort, forced it to slide open. She was met with stale, dusty air. She aimed the beam into the theatre, scanning the dark shapes of wooden folding chairs in tidy rows, the old wooden stage cluttered with old backdrops, the curtains bunched at the sides of the stage.

Then.

A woman.

Alexandra started, banging her head on the window frame and dropping the flashlight into the theatre where it clattered and blinked off. Alexandra gazed down into the darkness where the woman had been sitting.

Alexandra ducked below the window, knocking the bowl off the counter so it clattered to the floor and commenced spinning around noisily on its rim in tighter and tighter circles, finally settling to a stop.

Alexandra shook her head, knowing that there was nothing to do than face up to it. She rose and turned to take another look through the window. Though it was too dark to make out a face, Alexandra could see the woman had turned to look directly at her.

"Hello!" Alexandra called. "Um, how did you get in there?"

The woman below remained silent.

"I, uh, I don't have a working key and this is my place," Alexandra said. "I'm Tabitha's niece."

No response or even slightest gesture from the woman below.

"Tabitha, the woman who owned the shop before me," Alexandra said. "Did you know her?"

Alexandra was quickly running out of nerve and small talk.

"I don't mind you being in there, but if you could let me know how you got in, I'd really appreciate it," Alexandra said. "I just don't like the idea of people roaming around my place, you know."

The woman turned back to look at the stage.

"So, um, if I come down to the doors," Alexandra said, "could you let me in?"

Alexandra waited for the woman to respond, though she suspected she wouldn't.

"Right, I'm coming down," Alexandra said, then hurried across her small loft, down the weary staircase, and to the doors. She knocked firmly. She knocked again. She listened. She knocked once more, then listened. No sounds of footsteps or rustling around.

"Let me in, please!" Alexandra called through the door. "I don't want to make a big deal out of this. I just want to talk."

Alexandra knocked a final time, waited, then rushed back up the stairs, across her loft, and to the window.

The woman was gone.

"Hello?" Alexandra called. "Are you still down there?"

She scanned the darkened theatre, looking for movement, a door, anything. *Had she been there at all?*

"Nope," Alexandra said, shutting the window. "Not doing this."

She crossed through her loft, went back downstairs, then

began stacking books from a bookcase onto the floor. Once the bookcase was empty, she pushed it to the theatre doors and began replacing the books until it was so heavy, there would be no coming or going.

She started at a knock, but it was coming from the front door. She hopped up and down to bleed off the spiking adrenaline, gave a manic little laugh, then powerwalked to the front door where Reeves and Róisín stood with beaming smiles and oven mitts gripping covered dishes.

"How are—" Reeves began.

"Good, can we eat at your place?" Alexandra said, slipping out of the bookshop and closing the door firmly behind her. She locked it, but instead of walking across the street to the Reeves's, she moved to the alleyway between the theatre and the neighboring brownstone. She looked back at the confused Reeves and Róisín, then gestured for them to follow. Which they did.

They skirted down the alleyway as a group. Alexandra's skin prickled and her muscles coiled, ready to attack or flee or jump or whatever needed to happen.

They followed the brick wall along to the back where a lane passed between the backyards of the houses and ended at the theatre. Behind the theatre was only more brick wall. No back entrance.

"This can't be right," Alexandra said, walking around the back towards the side street. There was no second entrance on that side of the building either. "This . . ." Alexandra muttered, looking around the building. "How?"

"Are you feeling okay?" Róisín asked.

"Sure, yeah," Alexandra said, forcing a smile. "Just hungry, so shall we?"

Alexandra walked across the street to the Reeves's. The elderly couple hurried to follow.

The three-story brownstone was narrow, but still roomy, with ancient furniture accumulated throughout the couple's forty plus years of marriage bought for a succession of three homes on two continents.

"We settled here about fifteen years back," Róisín said. "First visited to see those pink roses, you know. Reeves here was silly about his garden."

"Aye, back in Donegal," Reeves said. "Still miss it from time to time, but the missus and I needed a change."

"You don't have a garden here?" Alexandra asked, then discreetly glanced back at the bookshop. It seemed empty.

"Are you okay, dear?" Róisín asked.

"Yeah, of course," Alexandra said, then turned her attention to Reeves. "So, how do you manage without a garden to be silly about?"

"Oh, I have the biggest garden of gardens," Reeves said proudly. "I help with the roses."

"He's worked himself up to Second Tender," Róisín said, patting Reeves's hand. "Quite a feat for someone not born into the role."

Alexandra smiled, nodding her head to show she was impressed, though she had no idea what a Second Tender did, let alone why a First Tender would need a second. She looked back to the bookshop window.

Róisín and Reeves glanced at each other.

"Oh, I meant to ask," Róisín said, "a few of the gals and I'd be interested in a little book club once your shop is on its legs again? How would that sound?"

Alexandra pried her attention back to her hosts. "Sure, of course. There's a plan afoot to remake the bookshop. I'll be ready to host all sorts of to-dos once the dust settles."

"Oh, that's lovely," Róisín said. "We're starved for culture."

"We've got the tavern, love," Reeves said.

Róisín gave her husband a withering glare and he smiled a bit too sweetly, as teasing husbands often do.

"So," Alexandra began, pulling the conversation to less testy matters. "Where are these rose gardens? I read about them as I was traveling in and saw roses during the funeral march, but I've never actually seen a rose growing anywhere."

"Well, as Second Tender I happen to have certain privileges, so I'm sure a tour can be arranged," Reeves said.

Alexandra laughed, then speared a bit of cod with her fork. She aimed it at Reeves. "Why is everything in this town so cryptic?"

Reeves shrugged.

"It's a lot to explain," Róisín said. "Everything, the entire town. It's all so different from the rest of the world and some things just have to be experienced first."

Alexandra moved the fork to her mouth and chewed. She considered the bookshop again.

"Do you happen to know how to get into the theatre in the back?" Alexandra asked. "I tried my key on the doors leading into the theatre, but they didn't work. There's no side entrance or any other way to get in. Also, a theatre without an emergency exit is a little frightening."

Reeves and Róisín passed knowing looks.

"Lass," Reeves began, "there's only sad memories on that stage. It was closed for a reason."

Alexandra's eyes widened.

"Oh, nothing for you to worry about," Reeves said, covering. "Nothing dark or disturbing. Just sad. The town lost one of its own, is all, and it threw a shroud over the town."

"That's why dear Tabitha converted it to a bookstore when she moved here," Róisín said. "It was a relief. Before her, the building had just been a shell where sorrow lived."

Alexandra nodded, then looked back at the bookshop. "So, what I'm hearing is there is a ghost in the theatre."

"A ghost?" Róisín laughed. "Oh, goodness no."

"The person who passed away, they died far, far away," Reeves said. "It's not their ghost haunting that building, only their memory."

Alexandra nodded, thinking of what she'd seen—a woman facing the stage. Clearly a woman. *Right?* A woman who was there one moment, gone the next. No shuffling feet through the theatre. No door opening. No door closing. But she had been there. *Right?*

She forked more cod and took a bite and chewed thoughtfully.

"Am I safe?" Alexandra asked.

Róisín smiled, took Alexandra's hand in both of his. "Yes. Safer here than anywhere out there in the rest of the world. The Town Where All Things Are Possible is a silly place and it has plenty of mysteries, but danger is rare. None of us understand the magic of this town, not even your fella with all his notecards. We've just come to accept it. Appreciate it."

"That bookshop of yours is beloved by this community," Reeves said. "It's a big place, and I can understand why it could be a little eerie, but it's safe. Not a single person has an ill wish against it. Just some are sad when they think of what it once was. That's all. In the morning, I'd be happy to crack that door open so you can get a good look inside the theatre. If it'd put your mind to rest."

Alexandra considered. There had been someone in her home. She knew it wasn't her imagination. The woman had found her way in; she might still be there. Either way, she found a secret entrance. If that woman knew it existed, then who else?

"Would you like to stay in our spare bedroom tonight?" Róisín asked, sensing Alexandra's turmoil.

"Yeah," Alexandra said. "I think I might."

Reeves pushed himself up from the table. "I'll get the bed ready right now."

Róisín patted Alexandra's hand. "I won't be one of those people who tells you it's all in your head. If you aren't certain about something, you should listen to yourself. We're happy to host you, but just don't give up on the town quite yet."

"I appreciate it," Alexandra said.

Róisín collected the dishes and retreated to the kitchen. Alexandra kept her eyes on the bookshop. She wasn't ready to run. She would not be chased from her new home.

In The Town Where All Things Are Possible,

Alexandra woke in a cozy guest bedroom filled with photos of children, grandchildren, and long-ago friends. There was Reeves standing on an impossibly green golf course with the Atlantic Ocean in the distance. There was Róisín in a pub, surrounded by charming faces with a banner reading "Farewell, Old Friends." There was a small home with a wall coated in ivy, with forty people huddled in tight.

They'd left so many people behind, Alexandra thought.

The bookshelves in the guest bedroom were Reeves's and focused mainly on sports philosophy, with every third book about boxing. Above the bed, where a crucifix might hang in a devout home, were a pair of battered boxing gloves with a signature. Though Alexandra stood on the bed to read the autograph, it was too looping and rushed to decipher.

Then a strange sound emanated from outside. *A horn. A violin. Tuning. A piano? A piano outside on the street?* Then a tinny hum. Then . . .

VOICES. SO MANY VOICES.

Alexandra hopped off the bed and opened a set of blinds. Outside was the town. All of it. Hundreds of them, all standing before the bookshop with instruments of all sorts.

Clack, clack, clack went a baton tapping on a podium with a grand piano sitting next to it. The pianist faced away and wore a quirky top hat. He then began playing a lovely, familiar melody. One that always brought her aunt's memory to mind.

And then Gabriel stepped out of the crowd. In a voice gifted by the heavens, he sang:

When you're weary
Feeling small
When tears are in your eyes
I will dry them all

And all together, every resident, in one voice and in perfect harmony:

I'm on your side

Alexandra's breath caught; tears dripped from her eyes. The pianist looked up at her and she saw that it was, of course, Jeffrey.

The Greek joined Gabriel, their voices a step to the side of each other's, but harmonizing perfectly as two who've sung together for lifetimes.

Oh, when times get rough
And friends just can't be found

And all together, everyone:

Like a bridge over troubled water
I will lay me down

Then only Gabriel:

Like a bridge over troubled water
I will lay me down

Alexandra realized she'd never been serenaded until this moment. And why not? It was something anyone who cared could have done. So easy. And yet it had taken until this moment, until this town, until Jeffrey, that someone thought to.

She hurried from the window, dressed quickly, and rushed down the stairs where Reeves and Róisín stood by the open door to the street, smiling, singing:

> *Sail on, silver girl*
> *Sail on by*

They sang:

> *Your time has come to shine*
> *All your dreams are on their way*

And all together, each of them in a resonance that shook the ground beneath Alexandra:

> *See how they shine*

Róisín took Alexandra's hand and led her out into the street, amidst the people. There was Noah the Actual Sailor with a fiddle, there was Tessa, her arms folded in front of her and one eye closed, and there was Wendy with a hurdy gurdy—of all things—and there was Jeffrey leading them all, playing his piano as if its very sound held up the sky.

Gabriel joined Róisín, Reeves, and Alexandra at the stoop. Taking Alexandra's other hand, he sang:

> *Like a bridge over troubled water*
> *I will ease your mind*
> *Like a bridge over troubled water*
> *I will ease your mind*

Alexandra wept and clapped and hugged her huddle of

people. Jeffrey stood from the piano and clapped for the crowd as the crowd clapped back.

Milda Gratherson clicked her walker up to Alexandra. "Well, are you going to open your store, or do we have to do an encore?"

"Could I have an encore?" Alexandra said, giggling and wiping the tears from her face. "I'm kidding, I'll open up now."

And she hurried across the street as the townspeople parted. A tap, tap, tap at the podium as Alexandra unlocked her latch and shouldered the door open. She looked back at the conductor, a petite woman with a short, serious haircut. She carried a baton and wore a sharp, fitted tuxedo. She lifted her baton. Jeffrery sat at the piano and began playing the melody to "Perfect Day." The Greek sang:

> *Just a perfect day*
> *drink sangria in a park*
> *and then later*
> *when it gets dark we go home*

Instruments piled up on the sidewalk outside the shop as the crowd swelled at the door. People walked in a few at a time. They soon filled the entire shop with energy and perfect singing voices. Books were lifted from shelves. Alexandra struggled to focus as strangers and new friends brought books three or four at a time to the counter. Tessa stood beside Alexandra to explain the strange functions of the register. Money was passed, happy faces beamed at her. Person after person thanked Alexandra for reopening Tabitha's store, then left to rejoin the chorus.

"Will they sing all day?" Alexandra asked.

"They will sing until it's time to stop," Tessa said, yet another cryptic answer. "It can get tiring."

Alexandra laughed, then turned to the next customer, then the next, then the next. Each member of the town came through the shop, even Elena the seamstress.

"There are many pictures," Elena said sternly, passing over a book of European tapestries, a travel log of Central America, and a beginner's guide to astrology.

"Still counts," Alexandra said. "And if you finish the one on astrology, maybe you can explain it to me. I've always been curious."

"Yes, but you must let me fix that blouse," Elena said, then walked back out of the shop.

Alexandra looked at her blouse, which she considered one of the nicest pieces of clothing she owned. "Whats," she began as she looked over the hem and the buttons and the way it hung, "wrong with it?"

She looked up at Tessa, helpless. Tess said, "You should. Elena is quite good."

And on it went, people filing in, steadily emptying the shelves, picking over the massive collection, then returning outside to rejoin the choir.

Within two hours, Alexandra was a whiz on the register and bursting with adrenaline. The crowd outside was thinning as the residents returned to their lives. Gabriel, the Greek, and Jeffrey still made music. Every song felt pulled from her own life's playlist: *My Sweet Lord*, *This Too Shall Pass*, *Anna Please Don't Go*, *Lifting the Sea*.

Then came Wendy, then came a happy young couple

she'd never met who bought out the shop's baby books, then came Dajuan from The Tavern Where All Things Are Possible, then came Leo, then came Noah the Actual Sailor.

"I think she loved you," Alexandra said, unsure if it was the right thing to say. "Reading everything she wrote. I'm so sorry she never said anything."

Noah held his books in his distracting hands, his clear eyes steady on Alexandra.

"I'm sorry, too," Noah said, smiling sadly, then leaving the store.

The shelves were bare all around her when Jeffrey finally stood up from the piano and led Gabriel, The Greek, and the conductor into the store. Jeffrey took off his top hat as he entered.

"Anything left?" Jeffrey asked.

"Scraps," Alexandra said. "I've hardly stepped out from the counter. Thank goodness Gerald brought me food I could eat while I worked."

Alexandra looked all around her, the shop now just dusty shelves, the register bursting. "I just can't . . . I just can't believe it." She turned back to Jeffrey. "How did you make all this happen? So quickly?"

"We move quickly when we move with purpose," the conductor said, stepping past Jeffrey to hold out her hand. "My name's Margot Riviner, I'm the mayor of The Town Where All Things Are Possible."

Alexandra shook the mayor's hand. "Thank you for this," Alexandra said.

"No, thank you for taking a chance on our strange, little

town," Margot said. "I'm sorry it's taken so long for me to introduce myself."

The mayor bowed slightly, then walked amid the shelves to search for the scraps. Gabriel stepped around the counter and opened his arms.

"My goodness, your voice," Alexandra said, enfolded in his arms.

Gabriel pulled back and simply said, "Thank you," then went to explore the store.

Jeffrey stepped up to the counter and leaned over. The new couple with their fresh glowing hearts kissed a sweet, lingering kiss.

"I'm so tired," Alexandra said, chuckling. "It's barely noon."

"Well." Jeffrey glanced around the store. "There's nothing really left to sell. You'll be able to start building your collection."

"But how? Where does one even buy books for a bookshop? Like, I've read a lot, but where do I find new books? I'll need thousands to refill the shop."

Jeffrey took her hand. "There is time. The town will provide."

Alexandra rolled her eyes, but then wondered why. Why couldn't she believe, just for a moment?

Because nothing is this easy, she thought.

"What?" Jeffrey asked.

"Nothing," Alexandra said. "Go see if there's anything left. I'm going to clean up, then sleep for a million years."

Jeffrey donned his top hat. "Oh, we have plans this afternoon, you and I."

"Oh, we do, do we? I don't remember being consulted."

Jeffrey smiled, then spun and did a silly little slide like he was in an ancient musical. He tapped his top hat, then explored the shop.

For the first time since she woke, she thought of the ghost as her eyes fell on the doors leading to the theatre.

Gabriel and the mayor plopped their selections on the counter. Purely random books on motorcycle repair, 17th century Russian politics, a romance set on a pirate ship, and a guide on how to juggle.

"Quite a spread of topics," Alexandra said.

"The pickings were lean," Gabriel said.

"You really don't have to buy the dregs," Alexandra said. "I've done just fine today."

Gabriel gasped. "And miss my chance to learn to juggle and explore love on the high seas?"

So she rang them up and thanked them once more.

Jeffrey reappeared, hands empty.

"There's literally nothing left," he said. "I'll owe you."

She skipped and danced through the shop, dramatically climbed the rickety stairs while keeping a flirty eye on Jeffrey, swept through her loft and flicked off the marquee. She reappeared at the railing.

"Lock that door and get up here, I've plans of my own," Alexandra said.

"Oh, did you? I don't remember being consulted."

Jeffrey locked the door.

Outside, she saw the thin teenager who'd she met hauling trash around town with his rocket bicycle. He was tethering the piano to his bike as others watched and offered unsolicited advice, which the teenager ignored. Satisfied, the teenager hopped onto his bike. Jeffrey waved and the teenager gave a casual salute, then pumped his legs to get the heavy piano rolling as Gabriel and a few others pushed from behind. Jeffrey flipped the sign to closed, then joined Alexandra in the loft above.

All those pretty pink roses

In The Town Where All Things Are Possible,

Jeffrey led Alexandra past the northern edge of town, skirting the hills and winding down to a pathway cut into the cliffs overlooking the sea. Gleaming limestone steps zigzagged down, down, down towards the crashing blue waves.

Near the base of the cliffs where ocean waves sprayed up salty mists, the couple came to stone pillars chiseled into the cliffs, framing a tunnel entrance. Above the entrance was a frieze of the sunburst Alexandra'd seen on Jeffrey's ice skates.

"Are you in a cult?" Alexandra asked, pointing up at the frieze. "It's really okay if the answer is yes."

Jeffrey smirked and took her hand. They walked into the tunnel boring into the cliffs. The way was lit with iridescent lightbulbs and the air smelled of the ocean.

"Watch your step," Jeffrey said. "The original tunnel was naturally formed over millions of years, then humans came along and widened the passages. We still get a lot of flooding inside, so the tunnel floor can be slick as ice."

"Oh, I'm good on ice."

Jeffrey glanced back, squeezing her hand.

Alexandra ran her fingers along the smooth limestone. "Was this a mining colony at some point, the town?"

"No, not really," Jeffrey said. "We've always been a fishing community. Well, that and the pink roses."

"So why all the passageways?" Alexandra asked.

"To get to the pink roses."

Alexandra stopped walking and pointed up. "Flowers

would be up there, right?"

"Patience," Jeffrey said, and so they continued walking deeper into the cliffs, as if plunging through the stone hallway of an ancient keep. Side paths came by, exposing an elaborate complex.

"How many tunnels are there?" Alexandra asked.

"I'm too afraid of getting lost to find out," Jeffrey said.

"No one's made a map?"

"In the library," Jeffrey said.

"Ah, Wendy's famous library."

"It's quite something," Jeffrey said. "There are some old maps of the town and of the caves, but lots of the corridors are too dangerous to explore, so those remain a mystery. The ocean tide can rise quickly."

Up ahead, natural light crept around the corner of a bend in the tunnel. A breeze wafted by, bringing with it the salt of the ocean, but also something else. Rich, sweet, floral.

"No way," Alexandra said, just as they walked into a massive sea cave. Sunlight poured down from an opening in the ceiling of the cave. Vines of climbing pink flowers raced up the walls toward the opening. After a moment, Alexandra realized she was looking up at the source of the sunburst emblem, but instead of sunbeams shooting from the center, it was pink rose vines.

Bees buzzed throughout the cave, darting from bloom to bloom, not believing their incredible luck. Alexandra and Jeffrey stepped out onto a wooden pathway leading to a harbor protected from the churning sea waves.

"Hallo, miss!" Reeves called from a wooden seat suspended from the ceiling by ropes. He was pruning the climbing rose bushes with a bushel of blooms slung around his shoulder. "Welcome to my garden!"

Other gardeners were working within the cave, all ascending and descending on a complex pulley rig that lined the cave walls, attending to the town's celebrated pink roses.

"How is this possible?" Alexandra asked. "And don't say all things are possible because this, absolutely, is not possible."

Jeffrey lifted his arms out wide. "And yet."

Reeves loosened a rope of the pulley and slowly lowered himself down enough to take a single rose from his bushel and toss it down to Alexandra. She caught it, laughing. She breathed in the rose's rich perfume, then placed it behind her ear. Jeffrey led her along the harbor to a small sailboat tied to the pier.

"Shut up, really?" Alexandra said, smacking his arm.

"Really," Jeffrery replied. He stepped into the boat, then turned to offer her his hand.

"You never mentioned sailing as one of the fun things you do," she said as she stepped onto the sailboat.

"Oh, I have no idea how to sail," Jeffrey said. "I assumed you did."

Alexandra smirked. "You know me so well."

When the boat's puttering motor cleared the cave, Alexandra raised the sail and a gust snapped it taut as the couple was carried away to sea. The clear blue water stretched off into eternity, the boat cutting through the swells with ease.

"We could just go and go and go," Alexandra said, tightening the cord, preparing to tack back into the wind. Jeffrey sat out of the way, assuming he'd be called if his help was needed.

It was not.

Alexandra learned to sail properly throughout her teen years despite her parents' reticence. Into her twenties she found every excuse she could to spend an afternoon on the water. But never too far. She promised she would stay close for her sister's sake, even as her heart longed for the open sea.

Once Alexandra felt far enough from land that she could breathe properly, she lowered the sail and let the boat drift as they ate. Dolphins skimmed by curiously, sea birds circled. On the distant shore, Billy and his waddle of penguins dove off of rocks down into the ocean. They squawked a friendly hello and Alexandra waved back.

The tall cliffs rose high above, the mountains stretching ever higher. She looked back to the sea cave. She looked. She looked.

"Wait," Alexandra said through a bite of her gyro. She pointed back to the cave.

"Ah, you see it," Jeffrey said.

They both looked back at the bright limestone cliffs, the great cave opening. Irregular shapes in the wall, formed long ago but weathered over time. Faint, but still there for a clever, observant eye.

"Oh!" Alexandra said, seeing it, finally.

A goddess, mouth open and full of pink roses, calling out to the world. Her eyes were suns with rays shooting out in all directions.

Alexandra swallowed hard, then swatted Jeffrey on the shoulder.

"You ARE part of a cult!" she said.

"No," he said, laughing. "It's just an ancient mystery that died with her followers a long time ago."

"But the ice rink and the pink flowers and all the crazy things in town," Alexandra said, trying to fit pieces together.

"We don't know," Jeffrey said. "We're in a special spot. We don't know why it's special, but we try not to question it, and just be thankful for our luck."

Alexandra studied the face cut into the cliff wall. She took another bite of the gyro. Then drank some wine out of a travel mug.

"I saw a woman in the theatre," Alexandra said. "Yesterday. Scared the hell out of me."

She looked at Jeffrey, but he only lifted a questioning eyebrow. She wondered if she'd see some acknowledgment in his eyes, a crack in another secret of the town. But he was just confused.

Alexandra pointed at the goddess in the cliffs. "Think it was her?"

"I can't tell if you're kidding," Jeffrey said.

"I'm not," she said. "That's why I wasn't in my shop. I got the hell out of there and slept over at Róisín and Reeves's."

Alexandra narrowed her eyes at him, faintly nodding her head. He put the cap back on his wine mug and sat it aside.

He leaned close to her. They latched hands.

"You really saw a woman?" Jeffrey asked. "What did she look like?"

"Too dark to see. I can't find the key for the doors into the theatre so I couldn't go to ask her how the hell she got in. There's no emergency exit, no side door. Only one way in, one way out."

She looked back to the cliffs. "But then I see all those tunnels. Maybe she came in from under the theatre?"

"I don't know what to say, but I'm sorry. If you want to stay at my place tonight, you can. I have some work, but it shouldn't take me too long. First thing in the morning, we break our way into the theatre. See what we can find."

Alexandra nodded, then leaned into his hug. "I want to believe in this place, Jeffrey. I want to believe in you."

"But there's a creepy woman in your bookstore?"

"Yes! Exactly!" Alexandra said, crying and laughing at the same time.

Jeffrey squeezed her, pecked a kiss on her head. "I'd be suspicious too."

She pulled away, to look him fully in the eyes. "You're not allowed to leave, are you?"

Jeffrey took a moment. "You mean, like, for good? As in sailing off into the horizon and never coming back?"

"Yes," Alexandra said. "Or just for a month, or a week. Or a day."

Jeffrey dipped his head. "No." He looked out towards the horizon. "I have to be back home every night."

Jeffrey pulled her back into his arms. "If you want to leave, go out into the world, I won't ever stop you. Tessa and Gerald can help with the Wider World. They worked for Tabitha and probably know the shop better than she did. Point is . . ."

He took a heavy breath, then motioned to the sea.

"If this is your happiness," he said. "I want you to have it. The town will be here. If you want to just leave for good, if it's all too much, then do that."

"But you can't go with me?" she asked.

"I'm sorry," Jeffrey—The Man—said. "Too many people depend on me."

For a time, they only listened to the clinking of the mast, the water lapping against the boat, the distant chatter of penguins.

They finished their gyros and wine.

They watched the clouds roll past the sun.

They listened to the dolphins frolic and splash.

They embraced the afternoon for all the time it could afford them.

Then she raised the sail and aimed for home.

In The Town Where All Things Are Possible,

a small bungalow sat at the foot of a mountain at the very end of a winding road. There were no fences. A lone streetlight marked the end of the town's power grid with a single power line dangling down to the bungalow. Distant waves crashed like whispers from another room.

Behind the bungalow was a quick walk to the cliffs where a circular glass-and-wood structure sat just at the edge—almost a greenhouse, but not quite. Inside, the grand piano rested, facing the sea and the setting sun.

"You have a separate house just for your piano?" Alexandra asked.

"I'd hardly call it a house," Jeffrey said as he unlatched the glass door. A humidifier hummed in the corner. Alexandra stepped in behind Jeffrey and closed the door behind her.

"So here she is," Alexandra said, lifting the black, wooden lid. She pressed on middle D♭ and listened. In the small space filled with flat glass planes, she expected an echo, but the sound rang pure and lovely. "If I had a piano this beautiful, I'd build a house for it, too."

Alexandra gestured with both arms to the piano bench. "Well?"

Jeffrey bowed, then sat at the bench and faced the piano. He softly played a few chords, staccato, then a flurry of scales, just warming up. He took a deep breath, fingertips resting on the keys. "Any requests?"

"Dazzle me," Alexandra said.

So he did. Mozart's boldness, then Gershwin's playfulness. Next came moody, blood-stirring Beethoven. Alexandra sat at the edge of the bench and watched Jeffrey's fingers work, his eyes moving from the ocean to the keys, then back to the ocean. At times they closed, and other times they aimed up and to the right as he tried to retrieve music notation from his memory.

Then he jumped into a clumsy attempt at Leonard Cohen, laughing as he realized he'd forgotten more than he remembered.

"Okay," he said, closing the lid. "I've done enough damage for one day."

"You are quite something, Jeffrey The Man Who Holds The Town Together," Alexandra said.

"I must be, to get you to say my entire name."

She placed her hand on his, their fingers entangling. "Don't get cocky."

As she admired the piano, she sighed softly.

"What?" Jeffrey asked.

"Does this mean I need to learn an instrument?" she asked. "Since everyone else in town is so musical?"

"Bah," he said.

"Bah?" she said.

"Yes, bah," Jeffrey said once more. "Learn one if you want, or just sing when it's time to sing, or stay quiet. These are just traditions, not laws. I didn't even learn to play piano until I was an adult."

"Why did you start?" she asked.

He fell quiet. He opened the piano once more, releasing his other hand from hers and began playing distractedly, just a rolling and gentle improvisation.

"Is this the time to talk about her?" he asked.

"Who?" Alexandra asked, then "Oh." She looked at the piano, then at the room around her. "This was all Samantha's."

"Yes," Jeffrey said. "It was my wedding present for her." He continued playing steadily, distracted. "She was the best of us."

"And you took up piano after she died?"

"That's right," he said. "She wouldn't want her most cherished possession to be forgotten on this cliff. In this tomb where she'd planned on teaching our children,."

"I'm sorry," Alexandra said.

Jeffrey lifted his fingers from the keys. He closed the lid. "I'm sorry," he said. "This is a lot to sign up for."

"What?"

"A widower from a strange town pulling so much history," Jeffrey said. "So much heavy history."

"I'm a strong gal," Alexandra said. "I'm up for it if you are."

They sat quietly at the piano bench, the humidifier humming, the sun extinguishing itself in the ocean.

"Are you?" Alexandra whispered. "Are you up for it?"

Jeffrey turned on the seat to face her. He took both her hands in his. "I'm a strong fella."

Alexandra was relieved that his home wasn't filled with pictures of them. The bungalow instead possessed the absent-minded clutter of every other single man's home she'd ever been in. Magazines left where he'd tired of them, dishes piled in the sink, one sock of a pair in the living room, the other sock of the pair halfway in the laundry basket. Sheets in a tangle on the bed, art prints tacked crooked on the wall, the bathroom sink water-spotted.

There were photos of his family, of him as a boy with a black-and-white mop of a dog, him and Leopold standing with proud smiles on a rain-soaked golf course, mud splattered up to their waists while both leaned on drivers.

But nowhere was Samantha. Alexandra had feared his wife's face would glare from every wall—the loss ever present. She didn't want him to forget Samantha, such a thing didn't seem possible, just as she couldn't forget those she'd once loved. But it was different, she knew. He still loved her and always would.

She went to a window and looked back at the town, at the distant hilltop office with its bulb still burning.

"Do you have to go back tonight?" Alexandra asked.

"Yes," Jeffrey said. "Every night, no vacations. But it won't take me long. I'll be there and back in bed without you even noticing."

"What do you do when you go?" Alexandra asked. "And why so late?"

Jeffrey stepped closer to her, folding his arms around her. She leaned back against him.

"People don't understand what I do," he said. "And it's for the best. The more I can work in solitude, the better."

"So intriguing," she said.

"The reality is far more banal," he said, though he knew that wasn't exactly true.

Alexandra turned in his arms to face him, then pressed her finger on his chest.

"Is there room for both of us in there?" she asked.

"You and the town?" he asked.

One edge of her mouth rose with a half-smile. "It's interesting that's what you thought I meant."

"Oh, you and Samantha," Jeffrey said. "Yes."

"But what about the town?" Alexandra asked. "Is there room for all three of us?"

Jeffrey nodded, though he couldn't be certain.

A way with ghosts

In The Town Where All Things Are Possible,

The Man Who Holds The Town Together stole through the misty midnight air, completing his task in secrecy with only the community's marauding sleuth of cats to witness the strange ceremony.

When he returned to his home, he was reminded of the joy of finding another person occupying his bed. Alexandra slept soundly, her worries and doubts set aside. Jeffrey sat across the room and listened to her soft snores. They stirred old, familiar feelings. Vulnerability. Hope.

But he worried.

After a time, he cleared the tears and gently slipped under the sheets so that he could put his doubts aside. Just for a little while, just there in this reclaimed sanctuary.

Upon waking in the morning, Alexandra was stunned she'd slept through it all. She was certain she would've woken the moment Jeffrey slipped from the bed, and yet.

They skipped breakfast and walked back into town to greet Gerald at the front door of The Wider World Books & Novelties. He held onto a grocery sack with his portfolio wedged into his armpit.

"Wasn't sure if you'd be in the store, across the street, or other parts unknown," Gerald called.

"Parts unknown, as it turns out," Alexandra said, pulling out her key and shouldering open the front door. Jeffrey and Gerald followed her in, then Gerald sat the bag on the counter and began unpacking a quiche glistening in plastic wrap, a pint of milk, two hearty muffins, and a bunch of plump, purple grapes.

"Didn't know we'd be three, so I hope there's enough food," Gerald said, unwrapping the quiche as Alexandra retrieved plates from her loft above.

"The place certainly feels lighter," Jeffrey said as he walked through the labyrinth of empty shelves. Every book, no matter how damaged, how obscure, how unreadable, had been plucked and purchased.

"It's astonishing," Alexandra said as she rattled back down the winding staircase. "I'll never be able to thank the town enough."

Gerald cut slices of the quiche, then split the muffins into thirds. They sat on the floor and ate quietly as Alexandra tried to envision her new store.

"Hey Gerald," Jeffrey said through muffin crumbs. "When you used to help out here, did Tabitha ever say anything about a second entrance to the theatre?"

"Oh, my ghost," Alexandra said. "I'd finally stopped being deathly afraid of her."

Gerald looked from Alexandra to Jeffrey, eyebrows knit in confusion. "A ghost?"

"I saw someone in the theatre," Alexandra said. "Through the projection booth window. But the door to the theatre is locked and I can't find a second entrance. Since we can't think of another way she could've gotten in there, the only logical conclusion is she's a ghost."

"No such thing as ghosts," Gerald said, seriously.

Alexandra and Jeffrey smiled kindly.

"Well, that's a relief," Alexandra said, unsure of what else to say.

Jeffrey popped the last of the quiche in his mouth, then

stood and walked towards the theatre's entrance. "So, there's no other way in here that you know of?"

"No, sir," Gerald said, starting to stand.

Alexandra snapped her fingers and motioned to the portfolio. "Let Jeffrey work, I've gotta hold up my end of the deal."

Gerald looked from Alexandra to Jeffrey, then back to Alexandra. He smiled wide. "He told you his real name?"

"Yeah, yeah," gesturing for the portfolio. "Make with the art."

Gerald opened the portfolio and turned it to face Alexandra. On the bristol paper, a young, striking face pierced out at the world—androgynous, high cheekbones, fierce green eyes, and deep red lipstick. Brazen, almost unearthly.

"Oh, is this my ghost?" Alexandra said. "Please say yes, because she looks fun."

Gerald hesitated, then said "No. This would be the dancer you saw before. On the poster. Born Timothy Riviner, she went by Gisela when she left for Germany."

Alexandra grimaced, hating that she'd called the beautiful dancer a ghost. Hating how it clearly hurt Gerald.

"She's lovely," Alexandra said, then a thought stuck in her. "Riviner, that's . . ."

"Mayor's daughter," Gerald said.

"Right," Alexandra said.

Banging from the theatre doors brought their heads up. "You okay?" Alexandra called.

"Yup," Jeffrey called back. "Just working on a way in."

"Please don't cost me money in repairs."

"I'll do my best," Jeffrey said.

Alexandra looked back to the portrait, then flipped up the sheet to see one more illustration, this of Gisela again, but full-bodied as she wore an elaborate band director's uniform, but a custom feminine cut with a magnificent pink feather sprouting at least a foot from the hat.

Gisela bore the smile of someone who'd just committed the perfect crime.

"She's the reason we closed the theatre," Gerald said. "After she left, it just broke the mayor's heart. Broke it. Then Gisela died, alone, on the other side of the world. No one could think of putting on another play. About that time Tabitha arrived into town and the mayor asked her to convert the theatre into something new. Something different."

"Something without a ghost," Alexandra said.

Gerald closed the portfolio. "Like I said, there's no such thing as ghosts."

A loud crack and screech.

"It's open," Jeffrey called.

They stood and walked through the empty shelves to reach the theatre doors. They found one door handle hanging loosely, the door now open wide to reveal the dark theatre within.

"You broke my door?" Alexandra asked.

"Nothing I can't fix," Jeffrey said, then looked down. "Oh, look at that."

He knelt down and plucked up the marine flashlight Alexandra had dropped. He clicked it on but the bulb remained dark. He clicked it off and on again to the same result. He slapped the handle and a beam flashed on, blinding Gerald.

"Ahh!" Gerald said, turning away.

"Hey, easy," Alexandra snapped. "He's an artist, he needs those eyeballs."

Jeffrey, chagrined, aimed the flashlight into the theatre, then looked back at Gerald. "You okay?"

"I'm good."

Jeffrey held out his hand to Alexandra. She took it.

"Here we go," she said.

And they walked inside.

The light beam shimmered off decades of dust coating every surface as Jeffrey led Alexandra and Gerald into the theatre. A mouse scurried across the aisle in front of them.

"Eek!" Alexandra said, startling against Jeffrey. She sighed. "I really just said, 'Eek.'"

"Your secret is safe with us," Jeffrey said, then swept the beam across a balcony ringing around the second level seating. Ornate wrought iron staircases wound down to the first floor. Foldable wooden chairs formed two rows, the top rail of each chair bearing the town's sun icon on the back, the cushions greyed by dust. A forest backdrop and props cluttered the raised stage, as if the theatre's final performance ended abruptly.

"*A Midsummer Night's Dream*," Gerald said. "We were halfway through the run when news about Gisela came.

Council voted the next day to close the theatre until further notice. I was a tree."

"I don't remember any talking trees in *Midsummer Night's Dream*," Alexandra said.

"I was five, so."

Alexandra glanced back at Gerald, chuckling. "And I bet you were the best tree in the history of theatre."

"It's true," Gerald said. "I was."

A velvet red curtain draped behind the stage. Jeffrey aimed the beam down across the stage, then along the aisles.

"No footprints," Jeffrey said, then swept the flashlight back along the middle aisle, finding only virgin drifts of dust. "Where did you see her?"

Alexandra took a moment to fix the position in her memory within the physical space. She pointed to the right row of seats, near the middle. "There."

Jeffrey aimed the flashlight on the row and the cushions. He swept his hand across the dusty cushion, exposing an emerald green fabric.

"She was here, Jeffrey," Alexandra said.

"I believe you."

The flashlight beam landed on wooden double doors on the other side of the row. Jeffrey turned sideways to step along the narrow rows, leading the others towards the double doors. Once reaching the outside aisle, they found undisturbed dust.

"She was here," Alexandra said.

Jeffrey nodded, proceeding to the doors. He tested the handle and it swiveled and clicked. Jeffrey nudged the door open slowly. He eased his head into the new space, moving the flashlight beam into the passageway with tables filled with fake flowers, scrolls.

Jeffery started and exclaimed "Ah!"

The other two froze, holding their breath, eyes wide and on Jeffrey.

Alexandra leaned close to Jeffrey and hissed "What did you see?"

He looked back into the passageway, relaxed. "Oh, right."

Only the donkey head mask, last worn by Gabriel.

"You scared the life out of me," Alexandra said, stepping past Jeffrey.

"Sorry, you just rarely expect to see a donkey head on a table."

Beside it were other props hastily returned to the table, expecting a next performance that never happened.

The passageway ran from the back of the theatre all the way to steps leading up to the raised stage.

No footprints. Not fingerprints. No sign of movement aside from the skittering paws of mice.

"That settles it," Alexandra said. "I'm spraying for ghosts."

"There's no such thing as ghosts," Gerald said.

"You keep saying that, but I'm starting to think you don't actually know."

"I . . ." Gerald tried, but dipped his head.

She looked around the passageway, the quiet, dark, lonely place where no human had been in a very long time.

Alexandra and Jeffrey crept along the passageway, then up the creaking steps to the stage. Their footfalls, loud as kettle drums on the hollow stage, agitated Alexandra's already nervous stomach. Jeffrey stumbled over a once-vibrant shrub painted onto cardboard, which tipped over and clattered.

"Oh, now you've done it," Alexandra said. "This is how people get cursed."

Jeffrey wiped the dust off his pants. "Not my first curse, won't be my last." Jeffrey looked up to Gerald and Alexandra's empathetic frowns.

"Sorry," Jeffrey said. "Widower's humor doesn't always land." He winced. "I'm just making it worse, aren't I?"

"Very much yes," Alexandra said, then smiled, offering her hand. Jeffrey took it.

Gerald walked to the curtain behind the stage, guiding it open, metal hoops scraping against a bar hanging from the tall ceiling. It brushed the dust on the stage as it opened to reveal a small hiding space for actors waiting on their cue. There was also a modest pulley system leading to rigging above.

No other doors, no trap doors. No other way in or out. Alexandra walked back along the stage, looking for something, anything, that could've been a secret entrance to the theatre.

"Shoot," Alexandra said. "You'd think this would make me feel better, but . . ." She looked back at the others. "I saw her." She hopped off the stage, stormed up the center aisle, then pointed to the row where the mysterious woman had sat, watching an empty stage. "She was there!"

She pointed up to the projectionist booth. "I saw from up there, clearly. It was dark, but she was real. I know it. There's a year-round ice rink, there are roses growing in a cave, there's Gisela's magical poster, there's freaking penguins. That's all possible, so this is possible, too."

She waited for an answer. "Jeffrey, this is possible too, right?"

"Yes, of course," Jeffrey said. He hopped down from the stage and walked to her as Gerald sat on the stage, moved his feet off the edge.

"We'll figure out what's going on," Jeffrey said. "In the meantime, let me get some supplies to lock this theatre back up."

"Something I can lock and unlock," Alexandra said. "I want control of this space."

"Of course," Alexandra said.

"Tell me what you need," Gerald said. "I'll go. Might be best if Alexandra's not here on her own until we get this sorted." Gerald then looked at Alexandra. "Not that, you know, you couldn't handle it on your own."

"Oh, I'm one thousand percent not staying here on my own anytime soon," Alexandra said, then looked at Jeffrey. "You're stuck with me now."

Jeffrey nodded. Pulled her close. "I'll need to thank our ghost when we finally get a chance to meet her."

The call home

In The Town Where All Things Are Possible,

a squat woman with a mop of curls tucked beneath a pointed witch's hat walked on the cobblestones using a crooked straw broom as a cane. In her other hand was a large megaphone that matched her black flowing robe with bright pink piping. Each step came with the click of the wooden broomhandle hitting stone. The straw rustled, mats of cat fur and bread crumbs waved in the wind.

She smiled with a child's eagerness.

Through the town she walked, tipping her witch's hat to all she came across. On the stoops of the town, residents brought out rockers, folding chairs, and stools. The Greek popped out of his store to offer her a gooey baklava, which she took with delight. As she paused to eat, Elena the Seamstress hustled across the street and nimbly pinned up the robe so it wouldn't drag on the cobblestones.

The witch thanked them both, then continued her journey as the streets came alive with neighbors setting out chairs and sipping steaming mugs of coffee. Careful parents slathered their children with sun block and herded them out of the witch's path. One little girl broke free so she could show off her new teddy bear. The witch booped the bear's button nose and giggled. The witch shuffled on, her broom clacking against the cobblestones.

At the Wider World of Books & Novelties, the witch stopped and faced the sea.

Alexandra was sliding a bookcase away from the center of the store, but paused to say "Guys?" From her perspective she could only see the broom, the hat, and the mess of curls flowing down the strange woman's back. "There's a witch in front of my shop."

Jeffrey paused working on the theatre doorknob to take a look.

"Oh, it's Thursday already," Gerald said as he slid another bookshelf towards the wall. "Where has this week gone?"

"Am I to expect a witch at my door every Thursday?"

"Not every Thursday, no," Jeffrey said, retrieving two creaky wooden chairs from the theatre and walking them to the front door. Gerald hurried to open the door for him, and Jeffrey sat the chairs on the front stoop.

The witch nodded kindly, then turned her eyes back to the sea. Alexandra approached the door to get a better look. Then she saw, all along her street, every neighbor sitting out in front of their home.

Alexandra glanced at Jeffrey as he walked back in, crossing around the counter to retrieve the stool. He paused to meet Alexandra's eyes, then looked at the witch, then all along the street.

"Um," he said, blushing a bit. "I know how this looks, but I assure you we aren't a cult."

"I don't believe you, Jeffrey," she said.

At this the witch looked back, eyes gleaming. "He told you his real name?" Then to Jeffrey, "I'm so proud of you."

Jeffrey nodded, his eyes down, thoroughly embarrassed. The witch winked knowingly at Alexandra, then turned back to the sea.

"Come on," Jeffrey said, carrying the stool out in front of the store. Gerald was already sitting on one of the chairs, but moved to the stool so that Jeffrey and Alexandra could sit together. Alexanda eased down on the chair, noticing Reeves and Róisín on their balcony waving down at her. She waved back.

Then from down the street came another witch, just as squat and curly-headed as the one standing in front of her store. Her hat and robes were pale blue with pink piping, matching her megaphone. Her broom was no less crooked. Light applause and whoops emerged from the crowd.

Then from up the street came a third witch in yellow robes with pink piping, and matching megaphone and crooked broom. More cheering as all the neighbors all stood and clapped. Jeffrey, Gerald, then Alexandra joined in the applause as all three witches converged in front of the store. They joined hands, tapped their brooms in unison, then walked up the street together, turning at the intersection toward the sea.

All along the street, the neighbors sat back down and waited.

"So, what the actual heck?" Alexandra asked.

"It's the Calling," Gerald said. "Happens at the Queen's Tide every year."

"Oh, that doesn't help me at all," Alexandra said. "One, what is the calling, two, what is the Queen's Tide, and three, why would a coven of triplets convene at my door on a Thursday at 10am? Oh, four, where are they going?"

Jeffrey patted Alexandra's knee.

"We're not a cult," he said.

"Nope," Alexandra said, swiping his hand off. "Make with some answers."

Jeffrey chuckled. "Lydia lives on the southern mountain,

Loralei lives on the northern mountain, Luna lives in the town near the cliffs. They meet once a year at the lowest tide in the place that is directly between the two mountains."

"My bookstore?" Alexandra asked.

"That's right," Gerald said. "Didn't you say you were already forming a bookshop coven? Here are three potential members. And they already have the outfits."

"Not funny."

Jeffrey shrugged. "Their family has been doing this for generations, Alexandra. It's not nearly as weird as it seems."

Alexandra stood and walked to the door. "So, let me get this straight. A family of witches have been meeting at my shop for some mystical ceremony and, by the way, there's a ghost that also happens to occupy my theatre."

"There's no such thing as ghosts," Gerald and Jeffrey said in unison.

"But," Jeffrey added, "the rest you got right."

Alexandra threw up her hands. "This couldn't be more cult-like!" She sighed, pinched the space between her eyes where a headache was forming.

Jeffrey patted the chair. "Stick around, you don't want to miss this."

Alexandra sighed once more, and with great dramatic effect, then returned to the chair. "If there is a sacrifice involved, human or otherwise, I'm out."

"Oh, we don't do those anymore," Gerald said.

Alexandra glared at him.

"Kidding," Gerald said. "Totally kidding."

"The Queen's Tide is an unnaturally low tide that happens once a year," Jeffrey said. "Before it happens, Lydia, Loralei, and Luna call all those we've lost back home to witness the Queen's Tide."

"There's no such thing as ghosts," Alexandra said with a thick layer of snark.

"Not dead," Gerald said. "Lost."

Alexandra then thought of the wayward note, the funeral, then the daughter of Mr. Witherspoon.

"The triplets are going to the cave," Jeffrey said. "They are going to call back the rest of the lost."

"And they have to come?" Alexandra asked.

"No," Gerald said. "Many never come back. Most won't come back each year, but they will at the very least remember us. They will remember that we miss them. That they are always welcome back, even if for just a day."

Gerald turned to Alexandra, a wistful grin. "We want them all to remember that we are, and will always be, their home."

"Even if the town isn't big enough for them?" Alexandra asked.

Gerald nodded.

And that's when she heard it. Three voices as if seeping up from the ground beneath them. Perfect harmony that stretched and enfolded and caressed like a mother calling home her children. Across the town, eyes closed, hearts stammered.

Alexandra folded her hands over her chest and her breath shuddered. Jeffrery put her arm over her, she leaned into him. The sound was stunning, in the truest sense of the word. There was nothing to do, but listen.

And for a time that seemed both endless and all too brief,

the three witches sang from within the cave of pink roses, their brooms held above their heads, the megaphones pointed up towards the hole in the cave ceiling where the sun burst through.

Calling home all who'd been lost to the Town Where All Things Are Possible.

Gerald brought out sandwiches as the neighbors began exchanging pleasantries and the children played in the street. Alexandra still hadn't said a word as she took the sandwich from Gerald and ate and listened to the town around her.

Finally, she found her voice, taking Jeffrey's hand.

"If I sail off across the ocean," she said. "If I leave the town behind to go see the world, will the witches call me home too?"

Jeffrey leaned to her, pressing a soft kiss on her lips. "Yes. We will always welcome you home."

In The Town Where All Things Are Possible,

the center of The Wider World of Books & Novelties was cleared, all the shelves pushed off to the walls. The atlas sat open to the illustration of the known world. Gerald and Alexandra stood above it, looking at both it and the floor.

"Lock is fixed," Jeffrey said, walking back from the theatre, but Alexandra shushed him. She held out her hand for him to take it, which he did and the three of them stared silently at the floor.

"How big?" Gerald finally asked.

"Big," Alexandra said. "I want each bookshelf row oriented to a compass rose at the center. I don't want just a copy of this map, I want your version of it. Whatever that looks like. Can you do it?"

"I can do it," Gerald said. He gathered the atlas, then his portfolio resting on the counter. He slipped out the front door just as Wendy the librarian and Mayor Margot Riviner approached. Wendy's keyring jangled as she walked.

"Oh, hey," Alexandra called, meeting them at the door. "Afraid you caught us redecorating."

The mayor shrugged, then took in the space. "It already feels lighter," she said. "I thought the world of Tabitha, but I'll admit I was a little intimidated by the clutter every time I walked in."

The mayor's eyes landed on the door to the theatre, the new brass deadbolt locking it closed.

"You opened the theatre?" the mayor asked, still facing the double doors.

Alexandra looked at Wendy, unsure of what to say. Then

to Jeffrey.

"We couldn't find the key to the old lock," Jeffrey said. "So we swapped it."

The mayor didn't move, didn't acknowledge, just stared at the doors. At the lock. Finally, she reached to her collar, pulling a necklace hidden beneath her blouse. She said, "I have the key."

At the end of the necklace was a tarnished key. The mayor took off the necklace. After a deep breath, she turned, forced a smile, then handed the key to Alexandra. "But you wouldn't have known that. I'm sorry. I should've said something sooner."

Alexandra folded the necklace and palmed it and the key, as if removing the thing from sight might make the moment a little easier on everyone.

"Yes, so," the mayor said, clearing a tear from the edge of her eye before it could smudge her eyeliner. "We're here to propose a book club."

"To get people in the habit of coming back to the Wider World," Wendy said, waggling her eyebrows. "And we have a name."

Dramatically, the mayor lifted her hands up. "The Book Club Where All Things Are Possible!" The mayor wagged her fingers and winked. "The tourists will eat it up."

"Yeah, sure," Alexandra said, hating the name but knowing the fight was already lost. "Um, I'll need to get some books in and get the store sorted. When were you thinking it'd start?"

"Next week?" the mayor asked in a tone that sounded awfully close to a directive.

Alexandra huffed a laugh. Then shrugged. "Sure, okay, no time like the present. Do you know what book you'll be reading?"

"Oh, honey," the mayor said, taking both Alexandra's hands in hers. "That's your job."

The mayor's eyes shifted back to the theatre doors once more, then another covering smile before she spun around to walk out the door. "It's settled. We'll have posters printed and get it on our newsletter."

"Perhaps we could get Gerald involved?" Jeffrey asked.

"Oh, fantastic idea, Jeffrey," Alexandra said. "Now I just have to figure out how to get actual books."

It was then she noticed the mayor's cold eyes on Jeffrey.

"You told her your real name," the mayor said.

A moment passed before Jeffrey said, "yes."

Silence fell on the group.

"I see," the mayor said. Her frown eased. Not anger. Regret, maybe. Alexandra couldn't read the mayor.

"Well," the mayor said, her diplomatic buoyancy returning. She swept towards the door, then paused to look back. "And don't worry, honey. I know it's short notice, but it'll turn out great. After all, just remember where you live now."

And then the mayor was gone, leaving Alexandra to look back back at Wendy and Jeffrey in a bit of confusion.

Wendy said, "She meant The Town Where All—"

"Oh, I got that part," Alexandra said, then holding up the necklace. "Why did she have a key to my store?"

"She's the one who closed the theatre," Wendy said.

"And what keys to my shop do you have on that ring of yours?"

"None," Wendy said, untying the bow and holding them up. "You are welcome to test them out."

Alexandra studied the keys, but didn't take them.

"You've heard about Gisela?" Wendy asked.

"She's seen the poster," Jeffrey said.

Wendy frowned, nodding. "Of course, right. Well, Gisela was Margot's son." Wendy winced. "Daughter, I mean."

"We told her," Jeffrey said.

Alexandra walked back to the theatre door, running her hand on the lock, the door. "The mayor closed the theatre after she died. And now I've reopened it."

"It needs to happen," Wendy said, following Alexandra. "Margot was so angry when Gisela left. Their last conversation was . . . hard."

Alexandra shook her head. "I can't imagine how hard that would be, to know that's how you left it."

"I'm glad you are reopening the theatre," Wendy said. "And in time Margot will be too. We can't lock up our past forever. It'll just be hard for her, so . . ."

Aelxandra nodded. "For what it's worth, I'm not planning on opening the theatre again. I just wanted to see what was inside."

"And what did you find?" Wendy asked.

Alexandra looked at Jeffrey, then to the door. "Nothing but ghosts."

"Don't let anyone lie to you," Wendy said. "This town is full of ghosts. But so is everywhere else."

Alexandra held up the necklace again, examining the key. She put it in her pocket, then turned to Wendy. "So, about that library of yours."

In The Town Where All Things Are Possible,

a gravel path led out the southwestern edge of the town border, up along a twin mountain base, climbing and curving until, finally, it reached a brick structure sprouting just at the point where the base ended and a steep slope began.

The library was true to Gerald's sketch, a brick silo rising three stories from its rocky perch. Alexandra could've walked past it dozens of times and assumed it was either an old military structure or a horrid experiment of brutalism, never suspecting it held an actual library. A short, rust red metal staircase led to a steel door. Without windows or signage, the library was far from the inspiring temples of literacy Alexandra had fallen in love with as a child and dreamed of visiting all around the world.

Who would want to read here? Alexandra thought.

She turned back to the town nestled below. A quiet cluster of brownstones, shops, and modest parks. Farmland stretched out from its center, then countryside off to the horizons. So much of the world had been absorbed by the sprawl of civilization, yet this picturesque town remained isolated. Another mystery to add to the many others.

Jeffrey's footsteps crunched in the gravel as he joined her, taking her hand and taking in the sight.

"Well, we've come this far," Wendy said, waving them to follow along the path up to the silo. She untied the bow holding her ring of keys to her belt loop, then picked through until she found the right one. They stepped up the rusted steel stairs. When they reached the top, Wendy slid the key into a heavy deadbolt. The lock turned with effort, then the reinforced door swung out. It was as thick as a battleship hatch, as if it had been fortified against floods, explosions, and nuclear armageddon.

Actually, Alexandra thought, *that's exactly what it is.*

She thunked her knuckles on the steel, then followed Wendy inside with Jeffrey right behind. The door clanged shut behind Jeffrey just as warm lights flickered and hummed, illuminating wooden bookcases, ladders, and walkways ringing all the way up the silo walls. A large, round skylight glowed above, similar in shape to the hole in the cave ceiling. Dust swirled in the sunbeams.

Then Alexandra noticed that there were no books. Only scrolls, rolled up and tied with leather straps. And there were thousands and thousands of them. The shelves were arranged in sharp angles forming downward pointed triangles, the scrolls then laying upon each other in heaps of twelve per shelf. Above each section was a yellowed, brittle sign.

"Is that Portuguese?" Alexandra said, walking across the silo to a shelf.

"Good eye," Wendy said. "Can you read it?"

"Well, my aunt used to say—" Alexandra said, then her foot landed on hollow steel. She looked down to see she was standing on the sunburst in the exact center of the silo. She stepped off to get a better look at the ornate, circular, steel emblem. She tapped on it again with her foot and it rattled slightly.

"That opens, doesn't it?" she asked, looking up to Wendy.

"Nothing gets by this one," Wendy said, grinning at

Jeffrey. "You have your work cut out for you."

"That I do," Jeffrey said.

Wendy pulled out her ring of keys, searching for and finding a long brass key with a thick shaft and a large bow shaped like the outline of the sun icon. She knelt down to the sunburst emblem and placed the key into a slot in the middle. The key turned with a hollow thunk, then a plate snapped open at the edge of the trapdoor, revealing a bar underneath. Wendy grasped it, then, with a grunt, she pulled open the trapdoor. It swung up until two braces clacked into place, holding it open.

A spiral staircase led below, where warm lights flickered and hummed to life.

"This crazy town," Alexandra said.

On the underside of the trapdoor, a bronze plaque shone in the sunlight that poured down from above. The letters were tall and serifed.

"My aunt used to say," Alexandra said, trying to drudge up her memory of a language she hadn't studied for decades. "Any sailor worth their salt can speak Portuguese."

Her lips moved, silently mouthing the words, trying to unlock meaning. "Sleep?" Alexandra whispered. "Until they." She thought for several quiet moments. "Until they no longer sleep?"

"Very good," Wendy said. "I'd expect no less from Tabitha's niece."

Alexandra traced her fingers on the debossed letters. "Okay, so what does it mean?"

Wendy knelt down beside her. "Do you ever wonder why, in mythology, there are all these stories of magnificent miracles with mountains moving, pillars of fire, dragons soaring through the sky; but we've never seen anything remotely like that in our modern era?"

"Because miracles were just humanity's attempt to explain natural phenomena we didn't yet understand," Alexandra said.

Wendy shrugged. "Maybe. Probably. But," and she lifted her arms to gesture at the silo, "the people who built this thought something different."

Wendy stood and motioned for Alexandra to follow. She walked to a shelf marked Amesha Spentas. "How familiar are you with Zoroastroism?" She took out a scroll and untied the leather strap, then unrolled it.

"Enough to be obnoxious at parties," Alexandra said, looking over Wendy's shoulder. The ink was faded, handwritten in a hurried, uneven script. "And I definitely can't read all of that."

"This is Hvar Ksata," Wendy said. "A sun god, one of many similar gods believed to exist by different religions around the world. Old polytheistic faiths had gods for just about everything like rain, the sea, sometimes even individual trees had their own gods. See this date?"

Wendy gestured near the bottom of the scroll. "That's 730 BCE, the last time they had a recorded, verifiable event from Hvar Ksata."

"Verifiable event?"

"A miracle, a sighting, anything tangible recorded by oral tradition or, in later societies, written down," Wendy said.

"So, they think this sun god fell asleep?" Alexandra asked. She looked across the shelves, seeing signs for specific religions, tribes, and regions around the world. "Along with all the others, and they built a library to record it all?"

"Now you know about as much as we do," Wendy said, rolling up the scroll, nudging the other scrolls aside so she could slide it right back into place.

"I was right all along," Alexandra said to Jeffrey. "Cult."

"The founders?" Wendy said. "Absolutely a cult. Their children? Maybe a little. But the grandchildren? Meh, not so much. And each generation that followed lost more of the memory of why this place was built. Now, a couple centuries later, we've moved the library from one building to the next because this is our heritage and it's important. We have some remnants of those Portuguese mystical traditions built into our customs, but something more interesting took its place."

"The ice rink, the moving poster, and all the other related weirdness?"

"Ha," Wendy said. "Yes, exactly. The weirdness. This town where everything just sorta works out all the time."

"Except when it doesn't," Jeffrey muttered.

"Right," Wendy said, then let the moment set. "Except when it doesn't. And we don't really know how or why any of this works, just that it does if we keep to the customs. It's why we're all a little odd, but we mean well. It's why some people feel they need to leave because our community can be . . . suffocating, I suppose. To some."

Alexandra looked back up at all the scrolls, all the gods and goddesses once thought to be slumbering somewhere out in the world, or maybe in the clouds, or maybe deep underground, or maybe in the oceans, or maybe in volcanoes. Then she turned back to the trapdoor.

"So, what's down there?"

"You're gonna be disappointed," Jeffrey said.

"I don't believe you."

"Oh, yeah, you are," Wendy said. "It's the town council chamber."

"The town council meets in a bunker under a library built into a whatever-the-heck-this-crazy-building-used-to-be?"

"One of the people who thought the town was too small left to become an architect," Wendy said. "He returned to build this as a temple of sorts."

Alexandra glanced up at the towering shelves. "It's about the most hideous thing I've ever seen."

"It really is," Wendy said, laughing. "And I have to work here every day. You couldn't give me just a couple windows?"

Alexandra examined the sunburst on the trapdoor. She walked to the opening and descended the staircase until she came to a wide, round room with lights humming all around, a round table in the middle with seven chairs. There were no scrolls. Just a bunker. A single painting of the sun emblem hung on the wall.

Wendy and Jeffrey joined her at the bottom, Jeffrey never quite stepping off the stairs.

"You're right, this is disappointing," Alexandra said. "So, the mayor and six others on the council? And they just discuss trash pickup and street signs?"

"Right, basically," Wendy said.

From above, they heard footsteps. "Hello?"

"Oh!" Wendy said, then hurried up the stairs.

The voice again. "Hello? I don't know where I am."

"Jonathan," Wendy said above. "You're in the right place. Come have a seat."

Jeffrey sighed, shook his head.

"Is that your dad?" Alexandra asked.

"Yeah."

"Does he know we're an item?" Alexandra said, waggling her eyebrow.

"No, and he wouldn't remember," Jeffrey said. "His mind."

"Oh, I'm so sorry." Alexandra stepped to Jeffrey. "But I'll remember telling him."

So they climbed the stairs and joined Wendy, who was tipping a glass of water for Jeffrey's father to drink. He waved away the water to watch Alexandra emerge from the staircase. Jeffrey closed the trapdoor behind them. Jonathan stood gingerly and took careful steps towards Alexandra.

"Good to see you again," he said, holding out his hand. "But I seem to have forgotten your name."

"Alexandra," she said, taking his shaking, fragile hand. "We met not so long ago, the day I moved into town."

"Oh, how about that," Jonathan said, he looked at Jeffrey. "And good to see you again."

"Jeffrey," Wendy said to the frail, old man. "Your son came to see you."

"Good, good." Jonathan leaned on Alexandra's arm, then said, "it's good to have children who will outlive you."

Jeffrey hesitated, then offered his father his arm, so Jonathan took it. "How did you get up here?" Jeffrey asked.

"It's the calling, you know."

"Right," Jeffrey said. "But the climb. You shouldn't expend yourself like that."

"My mind isn't really here anymore, but I'm not so far gone that I can't hear the calling. I will always answer it. My son would know that." He looked back at Alexandra with a kind smile. "It's good to see you again."

"It is," Alexandra said. "I've become quite fond of your son, you know."

"Oh!" Jonathan said, looking over at Jeffrey. "She means you?"

"She means me."

Jonathan patted Jeffrey's arm. "That's good, my boy. That's really good."

Jeffrey and Alexandra locked eyes.

"I'm going to take him back home," Jeffrey announced, then looked at Alexandra. "I'll see you tonight?"

"It's a date."

Father and son made their way to the door. "Did she say a date?" Jonathan asked.

"She did."

"And who is she?"

"Her name is Alexandra."

Jonathan patted his son on the arm. "That's really good."

Jeffrey swung the heavy door out, and the pair left, swinging the heavy door back shut.

"How did he get up here?" Alexandra asked. "That climb took a lot out of me, and I like to think I'm at least in decent shape."

"The calling brings back those who are lost to us," Wendy said, as if that answered everything.

Alexandra should've been organizing her shop, she should've been researching book distributors, should've been thinking of perfect books for the mayor's ridiculously named book club.

Instead, she climbed the ladders of the library and explored the shelves and shelves of scrolls. She circled the silo, looking from section to section, pulling out scrolls and trying to decipher what she found—gods from the Pacific islands, from southern Asia, from eastern Europe, from the New World. Tree sprites, djinns, fairies, creators, destroyers, tricksters, demons.

"There's no section on Christianity," she called down to Wendy, who was at her desk by the door, reading a paperback crime story.

Wendy finished her paragraph, placed a tasseled bookmark into place, and closed the paperback. She looked up from her chair and said, "This was a Catholic town, originally. Can you imagine the implications of suggesting the Christian god, the one and only god of their monotheistic religion, might be asleep?"

Alexandra scanned the shelves again. "Makes sense." She looked back down. "What about the cave? The woman cut into the cliffs? Is she a god?"

Wendy shrugged. "There's no section on this town, either. There must've been some local traditions, given how odd the town is, but you won't find any scrolls about it on those shelves."

"So maybe they were hidden?" Alexandra asked, eyes brightening. "The true secrets of The Town Where All Things Are Possible exist in some secret stash of scrolls protected by ancient spells and mysterious monsters."

Wendy laughed. "Should we ever have a spare afternoon, I'd love to join you on that adventure. But let's get your shop set up first. Then we battle monsters and ancient spells."

"Deal!"

Alexandra sighed and returned to the ladder. "So I may or may not have a ghost in my theatre," she called down to Wendy. "Who may or may not be a goddess. And if not a goddess, a ghost who's haunting the building." She paused, thinking of Tabitha, thinking of her sister, thinking of Gisela, thinking of Samantha. "And if not a ghost, then some underground dweller with uncertain intentions and a secret entrance into my home." Alexandra looked down at Wendy.

"Are you sure the calling doesn't bring back the dead?" she asked.

Wendy considered. "It's the Town Where All Things Are Possible, which means we really have no idea what is actually possible."

What is actually possible

In The Town Where All Things Are Possible,

Alexandra slept fretfully, thinking of the theatre. When Jeffrey woke in the middle of the night to attend to holding the town together, she brushed a hand against his back. He turned to kiss her.

"Sleep," he said. "I'll be back as soon as I can."

And so she tried. And so she failed. And so she rose to dress, gather her keys, and return to the Wider World of Books & Novelties and to all else the building might contain.

A chilly mist had settled on the town. Her footfalls were the only sound she heard as she walked along the cobblestone sidewalk. A glaring of cats watched from atop a stone fence, one turtleshell kitten dropping to the ground and padding alongside Alexandra as a noble escort.

And it did make her feel a smidge better.

She wondered about Jeffrey, about what strange customs he had in the town when it was only him, the alleycats, and the moon watching over his work.

She could follow him, of course. She could spy on his secrets, but she knew that was a path that only led downward into dark, bitter places.

She unlocked the bookstore and shouldered it open. The humidity had swelled the wood and the door resisted, but finally squeaked open. She closed it and locked herself in with the potential ghost or cat burglar or long-lost family member. Whoever it was, they couldn't be any worse than her college roommate, who dipped cabbage in mayonnaise and collected clipped toenails in emptied jelly jars.

Could they?

She took a moment to admire the wide open space of her store, the bookshelves still shoved off to the sides, the middle of the floor ready for Gerald's illustration of the wider world. She walked over to the center of the room and closed her eyes. She lifted a finger, pointing to her true north, a straight line from the front door to the theatre.

Nautical tales, fantasy, and science fiction would be there. From that true north, all other genres would orient themselves sweeping to the east:

- Dystopias
- Utopias
- Horror
- Westerns

No, not quite. She pointed back north and began again:

- Nautical tales
- High fantasy
- Cozy fantasy
- Magical Realism
- Science fiction
- Westerns
- Horror
- Dystopias
- Utopias

No, that's not quite right either.

- Nautical tales
- Mysteries

- Science fiction
- Magical Realism
- Cozy fantasy
- High fantasy
- Utopias
- Dystopias
- Horror
- Westerns
- Historical fiction
- Contemporary fiction
- Romance

Alexandra smiled. "And on into nonfiction," she swept her finger from east to south to west, "then into contemporary fiction, classics, and back to nautical tales." Her finger aimed back at true north. "But we need something else, for the oddballs, the books that can't be explained—just like this town." She pointed at the door to the theatre just askew of her true north. "Stories That Resist Classification."

Satisfied, she moved through the bookshop to her winding stairs, then clattered up the steps to shower, to change, and get some sleep. But first she went to the projection booth-turned-kitchen. She leaned over the sink to look through the window down into the theatre.

There, still facing the stage, was the mystery woman.

Alexandra's skin prickled as her brain cued alarm sirens. Her heart beating fast and heavy, she fought her instincts—run, yell, hide—and forced herself to remain still and wait for her mind to calm. She slipped her hand into her pocket and found the keys. With her other hand, she nabbed the nautical flashlight off the countertop.

Down the groaning stairs she went, knowing that whoever was in that theatre would know Alexandra was inside the shop. There was no surprising the stranger.

She unlocked the deadbolt, the clack of the mechanism especially loud in the surrounding silence. She eased the door open and stepped into the theatre, wishing she'd brought along something more intimidating than a flashlight. She used her foot to flip down the brass doorstop to let in some moonlight from the store's windows.

The woman was barely visible beyond the vague shape of a head and long, straight hair. Alexandra clicked on the flashlight, but didn't aim it directly at her. She was afraid of startling the woman, afraid of what she might do.

"Hello," Alexandra called out. "I'd like to talk with you, if that's okay."

The stranger didn't move. Alexandra took a few steps further into the theatre. She moved the flashlight's beam across the floor, looking for fresh footprints in the dust from the mysterious woman.

"I'm not a threat, I just want to know why you're here. My name is Alexandra, by the way."

Alexandra approached along the middle aisle, the darkness still not revealing any more of the stranger.

Then a squeak from below and Alexandra started at a mouse scurrying down the aisle. Alexandra looked back up. The figure was gone.

She aimed the flashlight at the seat where the woman had been, then down the aisle. She spun around. There, at the door, the moonlight glowing around her thin frame, the woman stood with long, straight hair and a tattered dress. The stranger stepped backwards into the bookshop and out of sight.

"Now you've done it," Alexandra cursed at herself. She dashed back to the doorway, kicked up the doorstop, and swung the door shut behind her. Back in the bookshop, she threw on the lights and began to search. She threw on the lights in the store, then scanned the clusters of bookshelves pushed away from the center of the store. She kept her eyes swiveling back and forth, watching for moving shadows, any sign of life. She walked around the register, flashlight held like a blunt instrument.

"Must be in the bathroom," Alexandra whispered, "or . . ." She looked up toward her loft. "No, I would've heard her."

She made another sweep of the bookstore and, by chance, looked out the front windows. There, on the far sidewalk, the stranger stood in the shadows, watching Alexandra. Alexandra hurried to the door to lock her out, but the deadbolt was already latched tight.

"Either she has a key or . . ." Alexandra didn't want to finish the thought. She hurried back through the store, up the winding staircase, and to the switch that turned on the marquee. She flipped it on, then ran to the edge of the loft, trying to see the stranger illuminated by the marquee lights. But the stranger was gone.

Alexandra went back down to look out the shop's front windows. She found the stranger standing further up the street that led towards downtown. Waiting, watching Alexandra to see what kind of woman she was.

Alexandra placed her hand back on the deadbolt latch.

"Well, what kind of woman are you, Alexandra?"

After a few seconds of contemplation, she made her decision, threw open the deadbolt, and followed the stranger out into the night.

In The Town Where All Things Are Possible,

The Man Who Held the Town Together admired the sleeping town through the hazy night air. From atop the hill, he could see most of the town. In every home was someone he knew, someone who depended on him, someone whose name was on a notecard organized in tidy boxes in his meticulously organized office.

In his pocket was a single notecard.

His gaze landed on the Wider World of Books & Novelties, tucked into a cozy street of brownstones. Its marquee glowed brightly. He was certain it hadn't been on when Alexandra and he had left.

"So you went home," Jeffrey said, uncertain which emotion he should give power to.

He began his descent down the hill, checking his pocket again for the notecard, and was comforted by the rigid edge of the paper. His steps were slow and careful on the slick walkway. He'd taken a tumble or two in his time. On his way, he passed the house of a puzzle enthusiast who'd once had failing eyesight, a dancer who'd suffered flat feet, two romantics who'd had trouble finding one another, a poet who'd recently recovered a lost notebook, a mother and father who'd once been diagnosed as infertile but now had two children sleeping in the other room, a singer who recovered from throat surgery, a husband returned from a distant war.

He knew their stories, he knew their needs. He knew they were just a few of many who needed him to make this journey every night. It was a privilege, not a burden. He was The Man Who Held The Town Together, and until the town gifted him with another role, this would be his life.

He could only hope that Alexandra would understand.

At the base of the hill he crossed the town square and passed the grocery store, which had once caught fire, and the pub, which had flooded after a main break. Neither showed a single mark from their past disasters. He turned just as he reached the post office, which had once been scheduled for closure due to politics hundreds of miles away. He crossed the town square to reach God's Blowhole.

There, he pulled the card from his pocket, folded it, and held it close to his mouth. The ceremony began.

The stranger led Alexandra through the town, skipping from shadow to shadow, never revealing any more of herself and never allowing Alexandra to get any closer than she had in the theatre.

By now, Alexandra understood the game. The stranger would not reply to her questions, would not explain how she'd gotten into the theatre or what it would take to keep her out.

The town slept as Alexandra and the stranger continued to cat and mouse towards the town square. Alexandra's adrenaline surged, but she held steady. She knew she must remain patient for the mystery to reveal itself.

At the bend of the road leading into the town square,

the stranger disappeared. Alexandra hurried into a jog to catch up; she slipped on a cobblestone, but caught herself on a brick wall. She scanned the square for the stranger, but only found Jeffrey.

He stood at God's Blowhole, silent, holding his hands at his mouth, palms together, as if praying. He was muttering something she couldn't make out. His eyes were closed.

She shrank back behind the brick wall and started back towards the Wider World. She stopped. She walked again. She stopped again. She sighed heavily, then returned to watch The Man Who Held the Town Together. To see what the stranger wanted her to see.

He continued muttering, eyes closed, praying hands at his lips. She realized he was holding something between his palms, but she wasn't close enough to see what it was. So she waited.

He opened his eyes and lifted his hands up to the stars. Then he knelt. He opened his hands to reveal a folded notecard. He slid it through the grate. He knelt and gazed through the grate for several seconds before standing and turning back to the hill. He began the long climb back to his office.

Alexandra knew she couldn't follow. She looked across the town square in hopes of finding the stranger, but guessed that the stranger had gone once she'd shown Alexandra what she'd wanted her to see.

Alexandra turned back toward the Wider World only to find a man standing in her path. He stepped fully into the light from the streetlamp. His torn, frayed clothes dripped water around his feet. His face was brushed with constellations of freckles, and his hair was a wild mess like weeds sprouting from garden beds.

He said, "We have a lot to talk about, you and I."

In The Town Where All Things Are Possible,

moonlight splashed on the steps leading down the cliffs to where the ocean glowed a bluish white. The boy from the photograph led Alexandra silently down, down, down towards the crashing ocean waves. They arrived at the entrance into the tunnel and lights within flickered as they approached. Alexandra took a moment to gaze up at the sunburst above the entrance. The boy, now a gaunt-faced man with shy, brown eyes, turned back to Alexandra.

"I know how frightening this must be, but you can trust me. My name is Scribe."

"Do you know how frightening this might be?" Alexandra asked. "And your name is Scribe?"

"Yes, why?" He brushed his hand through his unkempt hair.

"That's really your name, or is it like how Jeffrey goes by The Man Who Holds The Town Together?"

Scribe's breath caught. His hand rose to his mouth. He looked through the entrance, as if someone was just out of view, listening. He turned back to Alexandra.

"Don't call him by his old name," Scribe said. "Not tonight, not where we're going."

Alexandra took a step back. "And where are we going?"

"Just to the roses, just to talk with some people," he said. "You don't understand this town."

"And you do?" Alexandra asked.

"Yes, though I haven't been back here in years."

Alexandra looked at Scribe's still damp clothing. "Where exactly did you come back from?"

"You'll get that answer, but you need some context first. Which you'll get, I promise."

She glanced back into the tunnel. She then looked around her, found a stone larger than her palm, and plucked it off the ground. In one hand she held the flashlight, in the other, a whacking stone. She felt better.

"Right," she said, tossing the stone up and catching it again. "You lead. If I get the slightest whiff of danger, I'm beaning you so at least we both go down together."

Scribe smiled, wrinkles cutting through the freckles on his cheeks. "Deal." He turned to the tunnel and took a step in.

"He thinks you're dead, you know," Alexandra said. "Jeffrey, I mean."

Scribe paused, took a deep breath, but didn't turn around. "He knows exactly where I've been, but I can see how it might feel like the same thing." He half-turned, just enough to catch her eye. "And remember to not call him by his former name."

Through the tunnel they walked, accompanied by the sound of rushing water coursing through the labyrinth below. Alexandra gripped her stone tight and kept her eyes active, watching the tunnels breaking off from the main path, searching the shadows, ready to leap into action. The terror was exhilarating.

"Your name is Wallace, right?" Alexandra asked.

Scribe didn't answer right away, just glanced back briefly and kept walking.

Finally, "Yeah. But you shouldn't call me that, either."

"Why?" Alexandra asked. "It sounded like The Man Who so on and so forth only stopped using his name recently."

"Well, his role is different from mine."

"You are all definitely a cult," Alexandra said.

Scribe stopped. He paused. He turned. "No. Cults believe." He met Alexandra's eyes, a weary sorrow. "We know."

Even in the middle of the night, the town's celebrated pink roses bloomed vibrantly. The moon shone down through the hole in the ceiling as the boats gently swayed with the current, their hulls tapping against the pier. Torches burned along the pier and at the entrance, where Alexandra saw six townspeople seemed to be waiting for them. They wore suits and elegant dresses. As they got closer, Alexandra began to recognize them. There was the mayor, Margot Riviner, and the librarian, Wendy Fastly. Milda Gratherson waited with her walker next to Alexandra's across-the-street neighbor Róisín Reeves and Elena the seamstress. Jeffrey's once frail father, Jonathan, now stood tall, his eyes piercing.

"Hello, Alexandra," Jonathan said.

"You remember me?"

"Tonight I do," he said, gesturing for her to join them

near the pier. Scribe stepped out of her way, letting her pass along the walkway that circled the water in the center of the cave. The sweet fragrance of the roses blended with the salty must of the ocean water. As she approached, she realized the torches were simple tiki torches one could purchase at any hardware store, often at clearance. This disappointed her, cheapening the overall impact of the moment.

She also noticed they dressed formally, but in clothes frayed and dotted with little, long-set stains. They all fit well, which she ascribed to the talents of Elena the seamstress, but the clothes were old. As uncanny as the town might be, it was still a modest community filled with people with modest means.

Her fear eased. She knew them. They were strange, but they weren't dangerous.

"You brought a rock?" Mrs. Gratherson said.

"Not sure what I was getting into," Alexandra said, raising it and swinging it and the flashlight while growling "Hyah!" like a child playing at combat.

"Very good, my dear," Mrs. Gratherson said, then chuckled. "Strange person marching you into a strange cave in the middle of the night? If it were me, I'd have brought something more robust." She smiled and winked. "But you won't need it."

"I think I'll keep it," Alexandra said, glancing back at Scribe, wondering who else might be down in the cave, out of sight. "For the moment."

Mrs. Gratherson shrugged, then looked at Jonathan.

"Let me start by thanking you for being so kind to my

son," Jonathan said. "I have a condition, which you've noticed." He tapped his head. "It might seem like nothing penetrates for very long, but it does. It just lodges elsewhere and gets locked up. But once a week, all the memories flood back and I'm myself again. It is the town's gift to me."

"Six days with no memories is a gift?" Alexandra asked.

"Otherwise it would've been seven days with no memories," Jonathan said.

Alexandra nodded. "Well, nice to meet you formally." She scanned the townspeople around her, settling on Wendy's friendly face, which made her feel a bit better. "So, this is the town council? Any reason we're not meeting in the library?"

"We have something to show you," Wendy said. "And between a cave of roses and an underground bunker, we thought this was the less ominous setting."

"Seriously? Being marched through caves is less ominous?" Alexandra huffed, but then worried she'd hurt their feelings, so she added, "The torches were a nice touch, though."

"See?" Elena said to the mayor. "I told you."

Margot nodded, then motioned for Alexandra to walk with her along the pier. The rest of the council followed. Alexandra studied the fishing boats, wondering which belonged to Noah the Actual Sailor.

Jonathan pointed back to the cave's entrance, then to a place below, under the water line. "Do you see it?"

Alexandra peered into the water, seeing a dark shape. "What am I looking at?"

"His way home," Jonathan said.

Alexandra glanced back at Jonathan with a quizzical look, then over at Scribe, who still stood along the cave walkway. "You can't mean . . ." She remembered his soaking clothes when he'd found her. "He lives underground?"

"He's our scribe," Jonathan said. "Just as there's always been The Man Who Holds The Town Together, there's always been Scribe."

"And Jeff—" Alexandra said, but caught herself. "The Man dot dot dot, he knows?"

"He does."

Wendy stepped closer to Alexandra. "We were friends, the three of us growing up. We were born into our roles. The town thought Scribe was homeless, the abandoned child of transients, but his family has been scribes for hundreds of years, just as long as mine have been librarians."

"And our family has served as The Man Who Holds The Town Together," Jonathan said. "I'd hoped my son would've had more time to experience the world before taking over for me, but then my mind failed."

Wallace stood shyly at the water's edge, being spoken of but not spoken to.

"So, those witches singing in the cave forced him to swim his way back out?" Alexandra asked.

"Witches?" Jonathan asked, looking at the others.

"They dressed as witches this year," Wendy said, then turned to Alexandra. "They always do matching costumes. It's not part of our tradition; they just like to keep it fun."

"Last year I made them baseball uniforms," Elena said, a proud chin lifted.

Alexandra chuckled. "Wish I'd seen that." She exhaled

long and hard. "Why am I here?"

"We need two things from you," Milda said. "First, we have an open spot on the council. Your aunt occupied it until she passed. Second . . ."

All eyes moved to Jonathan. "We need you to promise never to take my son from the town. Travel wherever you want—we will help you with the store, we will hold your place on the council. We will support your relationship. Just, he can never leave. Ever."

Jonathan offered his hand to Alexandra. After some hesitation, she took it. He placed his other hand over hers.

"He loves you," Jonathan said. "He is lighter now than I've seen him since he was widowed. As a father, I am so happy that you've entered his life."

"But?" Alexandra asked.

"This town can't survive without him."

Alexandra slipped her hand from Jonathan's. She stepped through the group towards the edge of the pier, looking out at the ocean beyond the cave.

"There's a third thing, isn't there?" she asked, turning around. "It has to do with Wallace."

Faces soured among the council. Mrs. Gratherson glared at Scribe.

"Don't look at him; look at me," Alexandra snapped. "I already knew his name and I will call him by that name because he is a person, not just a job."

Mrs. Gratherson traded glances with Jonathan. He turned to Alexandra. "The reasons we do what we do might become clearer to you the longer you stay. Or they might not. Either way, what you call Scribe is perhaps more between you and Scribe than between you and us."

"Fine, we'll sort that out later." Alexandra folded her arms and gazed into the water. "The third thing is me pulling Wallace back underground, isn't it?"

The council members didn't answer, but their grave faces did. Wendy frowned, then looked away from Alexandra.

"I want to go back," Wallace said from the other side of the cave. "I do. It's not what you think it is down there. I'm happier there, and I'm needed."

No one spoke. The gentle waves echoed in the cave. A breeze whistled through.

"The Queen's Tide arrives tomorrow evening," Jonathan said. "The entrance will open again. Scribe doesn't need to be pulled or dragged or coerced. He can go on his own, but we would like you to accompany him."

"Why?" Alexandra asked.

"We aren't asking you to believe," Mrs. Gratherson said. "We don't want believers on the council. Believers can't be trusted to protect this town. To be on the council, we need you to *know*. And you can't know until you've gone down there with him."

Alexandra looked back at the submerged entrance, then at Wallace.

"Please," Wallace said.

Alexandra accepted with a grim nod, then tossed the stone into the water. The splash echoed throughout the cave.

In The Town Where All Things Are Possible,

Wallace walked Alexandra to the cave's exit. Above, the sky was softening to a warm purple as sunrise approached. The town would be waking, Jeffrey would be worried about her, Gerald would be arriving with paints to begin the map.

Alexandra would be struggling through yet another day with no sleep.

"So," she said, turning to Wallace. A yawn wiggled its way out of her mouth. "So, the Queen's Tide."

"Lowest tide of the year," Wallace said.

"Right. Low tides hit every twelve hours-ish, and we're a little past high tide. So we come back around early afternoon?"

"You'll know," Wallace said. "Then you'll come find me here."

Alexandra studied the thin man. He wasn't wasting away like a famished wretch who'd been entombed in the earth. He was a little pale, but not so much that his freckles had faded. His checks were gaunt, but not hollow. He looked as if he ate enough. Maybe not well, but at least he seemed healthy.

"No," Alexandra said, turning towards the steps and motioning for him to follow. "You're with me. You can go back into those horrid caves if you want, but before you do, you're gonna sleep in a proper bed."

He stood still. Alexandra turned to him, snapped her fingers and pointed at the steps beside her.

"I'd rather stay here," Wallace said. "They can't see me."

"Why?" Alexandra shouted, throwing up her hands. "Why is this town full of sad martyrs? The world doesn't rest on your shoulders, the world will go on if you take one day for yourself. This battered old mule act is exhausting, Wallace. Exhausting. So come eat some good food, say hi to old friends, and enjoy yourself for a few hours."

Alexandra descended the steps and jabbed her finger in his chest. "Your work can wait." For a moment she felt like she was talking to her father, to her ex, to Jeffrey, to herself.

Wallace considered the steps, then looked up the cliffs. "I never had many friends. Just Wendy, Leo, and, well, you know who."

"Jeffrey, for crying out loud!" Alexandra wasn't mad at Wallace, but he still winced as if he'd been scolded. She spun back to him and snatched his hand. "Up we go!" She jerked him along, up the many flights of stone steps until they reached the top of the cliffs.

All along, Wallace gazed out across the ocean as the sky brightened. Upon cresting the cliff face, the sun hit his face and he laughed, took a long, deep breath, and laughed some more.

"What was he like when he was young?" Alexandra asked as they crossed through the town, aiming at the town square. "Jeffrey."

"Happy, but serious," Wallace said. "He knew his future role."

The Greek fussed outside his store, setting out a sandwich board, arranging baskets of fruit, singing "Here Comes the Sun." He tilted his head when he saw them approach, studying Wallace. Then his eyebrows rose.

"You!" the Greek exclaimed. "Um, um . . ." The Greek snapped his fingers. "Wallace, yes?"

"It's good to see you again," Wallace said, his smile bright.

The Greek opened his arms and embraced Wallace, lifting him off the ground. "We all thought you were at the bottom of the ocean, the way you disappeared."

The Greek released Wallace and patted him on the shoulder.

"Well, I dredged him up from the ocean floor so he could say hi," Alexandra said. "Could you ask Gerald to bring breakfast for two to the shop? Oh, make it three, because I imagine Jeffrey's on the hunt for me as we speak."

The Greek's eyes glimmered. He began singing "Welcome Back" with his arms up, slowly dancing back into the shop, then bellowed, "Gerald!"

Wallace gazed into the grocery store, smiling. "It's good to be remembered."

"It is," Alexandra said, then nodded for them to continue.

At the edge of the hill, Tessa was watering her plants. Her exposed eye widened upon seeing Wallace, her hand came to her mouth, the water splashed against the pavement. Wallace waved, bashful.

"We'll be at the bookshop if you want to come say hi," Alexandra called.

Then they encountered the rockhopper penguins emerging from Leroy McMurry's long-unused tool shed, ready to start their day. Upon seeing Wallace, Billy squawked loudly and dashed, or rather waddled, with purpose. The other penguins followed, hopping around Wallace and rubbing their beaks against his legs until he squatted down to be amid them. Billy squawked and tutted at Wallace, as if scolding him for not writing home more.

"You were just a little guy when I left," Wallace said to Billy. "How do you even remember me?"

Billy chirped his answers, rubbed his head against Wallace, chirped again. Billy looked at Alexandra and nodded regally. He nipped Wallace's pant leg with his beak and tugged on it, pulling him to the tool shed, where he introduced Wallace to another adult penguin and two young chicks that were too little to make the journey to the ocean.

The little chicks chirped and danced, unsure of what all the fuss was about but delighted to be included.

In time, Billy called to the other penguins, chirped up at Wallace one last time, then led the troop on to their day's duties, whatever they must be.

And there was Jeffrey at the door of The Wider World of Books & Novelties, just as Alexandra expected. He was distracted by a notecard in his hand, but heard their footfalls on the cobblestones and looked up. He smiled gratefully at Alexandra. His smile turned to astonishment when he recognized Wallace. He shoved the notecard into his pocket, walked, then jogged, then ran and wrapped his arms around Wallace, who clung onto Jeffrey just as tight. No words passed between them.

Alexandra stood aside, not wanting to be a distraction. She cleared a tear from her cheek, then glanced up to her neighbors' balcony. Reeves and Róisín looked down at the scene, both with troubled smiles. Alexandra waved, and they, after hesitating, waved back.

Finally, Jeffrey released Wallace and took in the sight of his long-lost friend. "The calling," Jeffrey said, and Wallace nodded. "But why this year? After all this time? If you could come back, why haven't you?"

"I don't know," Wallace said. "It was all like a dream. I hardly remember anything until I was pulling myself up onto the pier."

Alexandra stepped around them and unlocked the door. "Gerald's bringing food for us." She shouldered the groaning door open and ushered them in. She waved one last time to her neighbors, then stepped inside. She left the door open and flipped over the hanging sign to Open, the whale's mouth open wide and eager.

Wallace was gazing around the bookstore, at all the shelves pushed to the side. "The theatre?"

"Closed long ago," Jeffrey said. "Alexandra's aunt came and opened a bookstore, then passed it on to Alexandra."

"But there are no books," Wallace said, grinning, confused.

Alexandra shrugged. "We're working on that."

Wallace walked towards the theatre door. "Why did they close the theatre? Some of my favorite memories were in there."

"No one told you?" Jeffrey asked. "I thought . . . the council?"

Wallace shrugged. "They tell me only what they want me to know."

"I . . ." Jeffrey tried.

"It's fine, you couldn't have known. But you can tell me now."

"Well," Jeffrey began, his voice heavy. "Gisela passed away. In Germany."

"Gisela?" Wallace asked.

"Margot's child," Jeffrey said. "They changed their name when they transitioned. Then they left, and that was hard. When Gisela died, the light in the theatre died with her. We thought it would be best to close it and hope something would take its spot." Jeffrey held up his hands, gesturing to the bookshop. "And something did."

Wallace nodded. "Gisela. Suits them."

Alexandra fished out her keys, then unlocked and opened the theatre doors, taking a moment to check for her ghost, thankfully not present. Alexandra held the door open for them. Wallace walked into the theatre, taking in the dusty wooden chairs and abandoned stage. He flipped on the lightswitch, but nothing happened.

"Sorry, I can't manage to get the lights on in here," Alexandra said.

Wallace smirked back at them, then walked along the back row. He used his fingernails to pry open a little wooden panel in the wall that Alexandra had never noticed. Inside was a breaker box. He threw a switch and the light burst on throughout the space. Startled mice skittered away into shadows.

"The calling is going to bring a lot of people back this year," Wallace said. "Something big must be happening if it managed to reach me."

Wallace walked up the aisle to the front row, swept the dust off a chair, and sat down. Jeffrey and Alexandra joined him, taking a chair on either side as they looked up at the empty stage.

"*A Midsummer Night's Dream*?" Wallace asked as he studied the props.

"That's right," Jeffrey said. "We heard about her death halfway through the run. We just locked the theatre and never came back."

Wallace shook his head. "What a waste." He then turned to Alexandra. "The town loves everyone who has called it home. Not just the residents, but the actual town. It's a living thing, in a way. And it misses us when we leave, so it calls us back once a year. I've always heard the call, but never with so much resonance."

"I still don't understand why," Jeffrey said.

"They've asked Alexandra to join the council, Jeffrey," Wallace said. "She's to accompany me back home during the Queen's Tide."

Jeffrey glanced over at Wallace, frowning, then at Alexandra. "They can't."

"They did."

Jeffrey stood from the creaking chair, stepped towards the stage, and placed his hands on the dusty woodboards. He hammered his fist down, then spun to face Alexandra.

"Don't do it," he said.

"Why?" Alexandra asked. She glanced at Wallace, but his face betrayed nothing. To Jeffrey, she said, "No cryptic answers. Be straight with me."

"The council—" he paused to consider his words. "I admire the council, they mean well. But this town pulls you in. The responsibilities, the burdens, I know you could handle them. That's not what this is about, it's just . . ."

"She doesn't like martyrs, Jeffrey," Wallace said, then gave Alexandra a grin.

"It's true, I don't," Alexandra said. "If this town needs help, why shouldn't I give it? Many hands make light loads and all that."

Jeffrey nodded. "Yes, true. True." He paced along the stage. He stopped, folded his hands in front of him. "Tabitha, when she first arrived, she was like you. She wanted to continue traveling, and for a time, she did. But then she joined the council."

"They told me I could leave whenever I wanted," Alexandra said. "They'd tend to the shop, they'd save my place for me."

"They say that, and I think they mean it," Jeffrey said. " But the town, it can be jealous and it will find reasons for you to stay. Nothing malicious, nothing dangerous."

"All the danger is out there," Wallace said, gesturing beyond the walls of the theatre. "In the world. It's vicious and the town knows it. It doesn't believe the world was built for humans."

"It was built by humans," Jeffrey said.

Wallace shrugged.

"What I'm saying is you want to roam the world," Jeffrey

said. "You want to explore."

"Are you saying the town will trap me like it's trapped you?" Alexandra asked.

"I'm saying it won't need to. Because once you join the council, you will trap yourself here. Just like Tabitha did. And I don't want you to ever feel trapped again."

Alexandra smiled. She stood and took Jeffrey's hands. "What's in the caves?" she asked. She turned to Wallace, who hung his head, knowing the question was aimed at him.

She faced Jeffrey. "What's in the caves?"

"I don't know. I was never told. Only the council knows."

"So, you just drop notes into God's Blowhole and never think about what's down there?" Alexandra asked.

Jeffrey met her eyes, then frowned.

"I didn't mean to spy on you," Alexandra said, holding up her hands. "But my little ghost led me right to you in the middle of the night. That's when I met Wallace."

Alexandra walked up the aisle towards Wallace. "Oh, and did you know I have a ghost?" She pointed at the seat on the outside aisle. "She likes to sit there. Do you know who she is?"

Wallace stood and followed, Jeffrey trailing behind. Wallace studied the seat, then looked back at the stage, then down to the seat again. "I don't."

"Do you know how she gets into my building?" Alexandra asked. "There's only one way in and one way out, from what I've found."

"You're right," Wallace said. "I started working for the Riviners when I was a little child, so I know this building better than anyone." He pointed at the double doors. "One way in, one way out."

"Which is a massive fire code violation," Alexandra said, folding her arms. "People tell me there's no such thing as ghosts, so how does she get in here?"

Wallace walked to the door and examined the new latch. "She's been here since you changed the locks?"

"Yup. Did you see her last night?"

Wallace shook his head. "No." He faced Alexandra. "Are you going into the caves with me today?"

"Maybe," Alexandra said. "Maybe not. I don't know. Why?"

"We might be able to find some answers if you do," he said.

Jeffrey approached Alexandra, lacing his hand in hers. She sighed, then glanced back at him, frustrated.

"I'll go with you if you go," Jeffrey said.

"If I say hell with this town and set sail for Tahiti, would you go with me then, too?"

Jeffrey shook his head. "You know I can't."

Then a voice from inside the bookshop called "Ma'am?" It was Gerald.

"That'd be breakfast," Alexandra said, slipping her hand from Jeffrey's. She walked past Wallace out of the theatre. At the doorway, she turned back to face them. She composed herself, forced a smile. "This can wait. Let's eat. Wallace is back home, and that's worth celebrating."

Jeffrey smiled and patted Wallace on the shoulder. Then the three of them left the theatre behind to greet an astonished and curious Gerald.

In The Town Where All Things Are Possible,

a caravan of buses, vans, family sedans, and motorcycles arrived from the countryside. As the roads couldn't accommodate so much traffic, the town's diaspora parked and walked. There were bright-eyed children carrying colorful streamers while being corralled by young parents, college students with their lives in their stuffed backpacks, elderly grandparents being met and escorted in by their adult children.

The town of a few hundred swelled to over a thousand, but just for the day. It was the Queen's Tide and all who could do so made the pilgrimage back to The Town Where All Things Are Possible.

And the diaspora was met with enveloping hugs and infectious laughter and pecks and pecks of kisses. From the horizon, more vehicles could be seen approaching, more immigrants returning home, all responding to the calling.

Within the Wider World of Books & Novelties, Gerald sketched out the world map on the floor as Alexandra and Jeffrey moved bookcases. Wallace sat on a stool and listened to Jeffrey's stories of their childhood, of marble runs throughout the town, of games of war with sticks and acorns, of a disastrous attempt to ride a bicycle down the hill. Wallace still bore the scar beneath his hair.

"My father shot out of his office like a coyote chasing a road runner when he saw you about to roll down," Jeffrey said. "But there you went, your wild hair swept by the wind, terror like I'd never seen in your eyes."

"Oh, I knew what I'd done the second I did it," Wallace

said, laughing.

Gerald had to stop drawing, he was laughing so hard.

"And you never even thought about jumping off the bike?" Alexandra asked, astounded.

"There was no thinking, there was only . . ." Wallace mimed gripping the bars and looking down in terror.

"'Oh god, what have I done?'" Jeffrery said and they all laughed harder. "And of course you fell and my dad fell and the two of you were just rolling down the hill in a tumble."

"And where were you, Jeffrey?" Alexandra asked.

"Running home to hide behind mom because it was all my idea!"

"You coward!" Alexandra said, swatting him on the arm.

And into this laughter Wendy walked, looking about with curiosity.

"The time Jeffrey talked me into riding his bike down the hill," Wallace said.

Wendy groaned, sat her bag down on the counter, then pointed at Jeffrey. "You were always a bad influence on poor Wallace." Then to Alexandra. "Has he told you about the performance of *West Side Story*?"

"You performed *West Side Story* in that tiny theatre?" Alexandra asked. "How on earth did you pull that off?"

"Creative blocking, and we merged a lot of roles," Wallace said. "It turned out pretty well."

"Until," Wendy said, then jabbed Jeffrey in the chest. "This one had an idea."

"Oh, you had input though," Jeffrey said.

"I said it would be nice if we made a moon for the performance," Wendy said. "That's all. Not that we should send poor Wallace, who, by the way, is terrified of heights—"

"Still am," Wallace said. "Probably more so after that day."

"Poor Wallace." Wendy caressed Wallace's cheek. "All the way up to the rafters to hang this moon."

"Which was your idea," Jeffrey said. "The moon, anyway."

"You're deflecting, Jeffrey," Wendy said. She looked over at him. "How long has it been since I've said your name?"

Jeffrey shrugged. "Too long."

She nodded, then remembered her place and riled back up. "This timid boy who can never say no to his best friend, Jeffrey, is biting back mortal dread as he's climbing up that rickety ladder."

"How old?" Alexandra asked.

Wendy looked at Wallace, who shrugged, then to Jeffrey, who said, "Nine?"

"Nine!" Alexandra snapped, slugging Jeffrey's shoulder. "You sent a nine year old into the rafters?"

"I was nine, too," Jeffrey said, wincing at Alexandra's sharp jab.

"No excuse," Alexandra said, then motioned to Wendy. "Tell me more about my boyfriend's devious and manipulative childhood."

"Well, to Wallace's credit, he made it up to the rafters," Wendy said.

"But I froze. I got my hands and knees on the rafters, but then I looked down." Wallace smiled, glancing up to find the memory, eyes closed. "If you've never looked down through rafters to a stage twenty-five feet below, you've never known true terror."

"And then?" Alexandra asked.

"I went up to get him," Jeffrey said, shrugging.

"You did, I'll give you that," Wendy said.

"Where were all the adults?" Alexandra asked. "Why did no one get an adult to climb up to the rafters?"

Wendy pointed at Alexandra while glaring at Jeffrey.

"At any rate," Wendy continued. "Jeffrey talked to Wallace for about a half hour, helping him crawl back to the ladder and then back down. It was impressive."

"I'm good in a pinch," Jeffrey said.

"A terrible friend, but yes, good in a pinch," Wendy said.

"So there was never a moon for *West Side Story*?" Alexandra asked.

"Oh, I hung it," a new voice called. They turned to see Leo striding in, then picking Wallace up off the stool and hugging him from behind. "I can't believe you're really here!"

Leo lowered Wallace to his feet so Wallace could return the hug.

"Where on earth have you been?" Leo asked.

"Around," Wallace said.

Leo stepped back to get a look at Wallace, at his tattered clothes, his pale skin. Leo's smile went to a frown. "Are you okay?"

"I'm great," Wallace said, looking down at his clothes. "I didn't really have time to pack. The calling, you know."

Leo patted him on the shoulder. "I'll get you some clothes. How long are you staying?"

"Just until the Queen's Tide," Wallace said. "Then I have to go back home."

Leo frowned. He looked at Jeffrey, who nodded.

"Nothing I can say to keep you here longer?" Leo asked.

"No, but I'm here now."

Alexandra pulled out more chairs for the group, but instead they all helped move bookshelves as they talked about the time Leo threw a snake at Wendy on a dare, when Jeffrey and Leo got locked on the roof of the theatre for an entire night, when Wendy got her first kiss from Wallace.

"Wait, what?" Jeffrey asked.

Wallace remained quiet, his smile bashful.

"How old?" Alexandra asked.

Wendy looked at Wallace, who only shrugged.

"You were five, maybe?" Wendy said.

Alexandra gasped. "Five?"

"I was five, too," Wendy said, defending her honor.

Alexandra gasped a second time, but for dramatic impact. "Again, where are all the adults in this town?"

Soon the crowds arrived and more hugs were exchanged. Wallace retreated behind the register as Tessa and Wendy helped Alexandra arrange the last of the bookshelves.

"If it's a bookstore, where are all the books?" a sharp-chinned grandmother asked as she ignored her high-octane grandchildren.

"We're working on that," Alexandra said.

More crowds came in as they surveyed the town and traded old, worn stories that still made everyone involved cringe and laugh. Many explored the theatre, reminiscing about the old shows. Alexandra did her best to remember every detail.

Wallace grew weary of the questions and the noise, so

finally asked Alexandra if he could rest in her loft.

"I'll take you to my house," Jeffrey said. "It'll be quieter there. I need to get to my office, too." He looked back at Alexandra with a grim smile. "I'll be back in time."

Alexandra nodded. Just as he was leaving, a woman with striking cat's-eye glasses walked in and placed a box on the counter.

"Hi!" the woman said, then exhaled deeply, wiped perspiration from her brow, and adjusted her glasses. She held out her hand to Alexandra. "It's good to meet you, Alexandra. I'm Denise. I was your aunt's sales rep."

Alexandra shook her hand, surprised by the woman's firm grip.

Denise patted the box and said, "I hope you don't mind me being a bit bold, but I put in an order for you."

"For books?" Alexandra asked, knowing it was a dumb question as she said it.

"Right," Denise said, taking out a pocket knife with an illustration of cat claws on the handle. Denise saw Alexandra looking at it. "Your aunt and I bonded fiercely over cats."

"I see."

Denise opened the box, then began pulling out books. It was a variety of adventure tales, many set on the high seas, all of which Alexandra had read and loved.

"You don't have to take them all," Denise said. "But I thought this would get you started. It's the calling, so you don't want to miss out on sales."

Alexandra looked through the books, brushing her fingers on them as if absorbing the stories she'd read before.

"These are some of my favorite books," Alexandra said. "How did you know?"

"Well," Denise said, pushing up her cat's eyeglasses. "It is The Town Where All Things Are Possible."

"Ugh, I know," Alexandra said.

"Sorry, I only get to use that joke once a year when I come visit," Denise said. "Also, I creeped your book reviews online since I first heard you were taking over."

Alexandra laughed. She patted the books. "A modest start, but it's better than nothing."

"Oh," Denise said. "This is just the first box."

Denise turned and waved in a line of people, all carrying boxes and sitting them down at the counter. Alexandra's eyes widened. "That's a lot of books." She looked at the overstuffed register, then to Denise. "Do you take cash?"

"We'll figure that out later," Denise said, then gestured to the town. "Welcome home, Alexandra."

The boxes kept coming and Alexandra struggled to formulate a plan of what to do with the clutter while the store was filling with curious potential customers. Tessa stepped forward and began directing the people carrying boxes to stack them behind the counter.

"You start opening," Tessa said, "We'll sort as we go."

"Keep the invoices!" Denise said, as she walked back towards the theatre.

"Right, keep the invoices," Tessa said. "Record your sales by hand and we'll work out the inventory later."

Tessa smirked, then lifted one box onto another, then pointed under the counter. "Box cutter is right there. Get to work, boss."

So Alexandra started opening boxes, as the store around her buzzed with life. Wendy and Tessa ran books to appropriate shelves as Gerald paused sketching so he could make a series of bookshelf signs. Alexandra explained the shop's new true north and how the sections would be oriented. She then dug through box after box, finding familiar titles that made her heart swell. She sorted them on the counter as Tessa and Wendy ran them to the appropriate shelves. Customers asked questions and made purchases; Alexandra fumbled with the cash register and took hasty notes.

Lunch arrived when Róisín brought a plate of her famous shepherd's pie. Several customers took a moment to take in its rich aroma. Alexandra ate while she worked. The boxes thinned, and then were gone.

"How does one build an inventory?" Alexandra asked as she flipped through the invoices. "Also what does Net 60 mean? And do I owe this amount or that amount."

Tessa plucked the invoices from her hands and put them under the register. "We'll discuss this later. For now . . ." Tessa motioned to a waiting line of customers.

Alexandra took another hearty bite, wiped her hands off on a paper towel, then got to ringing.

And so the day raced by, with hundreds of new faces exploring the store. Even after such a big delivery of books, the shelves were barely a quarter full and disappearing quickly as the diaspora cycled through the store.

At some point Tessa retrieved trash bags and a duster from the register and disappeared into the theatre.

Margot walked in, smiling a broad politician's smile. It

wavered when she saw the theatre doors open.

Alexandra waved to Wendy, then pointed to the cash register. Wendy cut off her conversation and took over the counter while Alexandra walked over to greet the mayor.

"People have been so curious about it," Alexandra said, motioning to the theatre. "Honestly, I'd meant to close it, but well, the crowd came so quickly that I didn't get a chance."

Margot nodded and smiled, her eyes fixed on the theatre. She didn't cry, but Alexandra could tell how hard she was trying to keep the tears dammed up.

Margot took a deep breath and blew it out slowly. "Keep it open," she said, taking Alexandra's hands and giving them a squeeze. "Keep it open." She left quietly.

Alexandra looked at Wendy, who gave her a grim smile. "She'll be fine. It's just a lot."

Alexandra turned to the theatre, thinking of the ghost, thinking of the generations of families who had walked through those doors, and of Wallace trapped on the rafters, and how it had all ended so quickly after a death on the other side of the world.

"It is," Alexandra said.

There is also danger in knowing

In The Town Where All Things Are Possible,

the tide continued to wash back into the ocean, revealing a little more and a little more of the stone doorway. Wind whipped through the doorway, whistling as it raced over the waters that flooded the ancient depths, turning and turning and turning until it found a way back out. It rushed upwards, twirling dust, then whooshed through the storm grate of God's Blowhole.

Soon, the wind went from a faint whistle to a deep hum, as if the world's largest horn was finding its tune. When waves rushed back into the cave to disrupt the airflow, the hum would stop. Then it would rise again, louder. The tide continued retreating, exposing more of the doorway, giving strength to the hum until it sounded throughout the town.

The residents responded to the clarion call. They emerged from their homes and shops. They abandoned their daily chores and cut off their catching-up chats with distant friends. They gathered downtown and lifted their voices to harmonize with the hum. Gabriel led, still wearing his painter's apron, white and teal drops on his arms, his cheeks, and his magnificent beard. His voice sailed into the sky and the townspeople joined, as if they were trying to summon a god from the deepest pocket of the universe.

Alexandra stepped out of her bookshop to listen, then threw a quizzical look to Tessa, Gerald, and Wendy.

"It's the Queen's Tide," Jeffrey called, hurrying up the street with Wallace in the lead. "It won't last long."

Wendy ran out of the store and gave Wallace a long, tight hug. "You come back to me when you can."

"I will," Wallace said, leaning into Wendy.

"Next year! And every year!"

"I will," Wallace said again, eyes closed as he savored the embrace.

Jeffrey joined Alexandra at the shop door.

"I've always wanted to see what was below the town," Jeffrey said. "I can take him on my own. If you aren't—"

"I'm going," Alexandra said.

Alexandra shooed Tessa and Gerald off towards the town square, then admired how they walked and chatted casually, as if they'd finally chipped the angst off their friendship.

"Okay, go," Wendy said, still clasping Wallace's hands. She grimaced, hugged Wallace once more, then stepped back. She waved, shook her head, then turned to join the town and all its visitors at God's Blowhole.

Wallace, Alexandra, and Jeffrey returned to the bookshop to grab a backpack Alexandra had previously filled with all they suspected she might need on the journey: food, the flashlight, a first aid kit, a screwdriver set, and a utility knife.

Alexandra locked the bookshop and they crossed through town on their way to the cliffs. On their way, Alexandra glimpsed the crowd in the town square, the immense chorus whose harmony could be felt on the cobblestones. Even the penguins joined in, their calls finding a place.

"My goodness," Alexandra said.

"Next year, we'll get to join them," Jeffrey said.

At the cliffs, they jogged down the steps until they reached the entrance to the tunnel. They hurried through the dimly lit chamber until they reached the pier. They passed by the pink rose blooms climbing up the cave walls. Soon they reached the pier and walked out to the end. The boats rocked and pulled at their tethers, waves crashing into them with a force only seen during the Queen's Tide. The usually placid waters now felt alive, feral, and unpredictable.

The doorway was halfway exposed now, the wind whistled through it.

"Once we're in, there is only forward," Wallace said, looking up to Jeffrey and Alexandra. "If you aren't sure, back out now. I'll be fine."

Alexandra nodded. She looked at the boats, then gazed beyond them at the open ocean. She settled on Jeffrey's kind smile. She took a deep breath, nodded, then peeled off her clothes, stripping down to her bathing suit. Jeffrey and Wallace did the same. They stuffed their clothes into the backpack and Alexandra zipped it up. Alexandra threaded her arms through the straps and clipped the front strap across her chest. Without giving herself a moment to doubt, she leapt from the pier, down into the water. As she swam towards the opening, she heard Wallace and Jeffrey splash into the water behind her.

"Be careful," Wallace said. "There's this weird vortex that can—."

But it was too late.

Beneath The Town Where All Things Are Possible,

Alexandra tumbled through the current that raced towards the doorway, then slammed against a flat stone wall. The tide thrust backwards; she flailed while the ocean yanked at her.

Then she collided against a body. Someone, maybe Jeffrey, maybe Wallace, clung to her with one arm. She emerged from the water into shadows, the only light coming from the doorway, which was now twenty feet behind her. She spat out the saltwater and saw Jeffrey, clinging with one hand to a steel pipe anchored along the flooded hallway. The water was at their necks; Alexandra's feet could barely touch the floor.

"When I was a teenager," Wallace called behind them, "when they brought me down here, the low tide was just over our feet. The world has changed so much since then."

"Can we make it?" Jeffrey asked.

"Someone with the council tries the trip every year," Wallace said. "It's not easy. And they don't always make it."

Alexandra twisted so she could grab onto the pipe.

"What do you mean?" Alexandra asked. "They turn back?"

"No, there is only forwards."

Alexandra thought it through. "My aunt?"

"She was the last to try," Wallace said.

"That would've been helpful information before I jumped into the water, Wallace," Alexandra said. She felt at her scalp where she'd hit the stone wall and found a welt, but no blood.

There is only forward. She used the pipe to pull herself against the retreating tide until they reached the end of the hallway. The pipe turned, leading them to the right.

"Hurry!" Wallace said. "Before another large wave comes."

Alexandra followed the pipe around the corner, where the last of the light was lost. They only had the sloshing of the tidewaters to hint at what was to come. She thought of the flashlight, but didn't want to risk losing it. If the way was only forward, she wouldn't need light to find it.

A roar approached from behind them.

"Hold on!" Jeffrey said, pulling himself closer to Alexandra and wrapping an arm around her.

Waters surged through the chamber, whipping the group forward. The chamber filled completely; they were submerged and yanked and pulled by the current, but they all managed to hold onto the pipe. The waters surged backwards, trying to rip the three explorers free to pull them backwards.

But their grips held, and the waters finally settled. Alexandra led them further into the pitch black.

"She said you were too much like her," Wallace said. "Tabitha. She said that you were also too much like your father. Duty and curiosity would pull you in two directions for your entire life. She hoped that curiosity would one day win out."

"Did she know about my sister?" Alexandra asked. "That she passed away."

"Yes," Wallace said.

Another surge of water swept by, but this one was gentler; it only lifted them up and pulled them forward.

They continued on.

"Why didn't she ever write?" Alexandra asked, shivering. "Why didn't she come for the funeral? Why didn't she ever come for me?"

"Your parents," Wallace said, as if that answered everything.

And to Alexandra, it did.

"How much further?" Jeffrey asked.

"I . . . uh," Wallace said. "I'm not sure. It's been two decades. There is a lever or something."

The pipe gave under Alexandra's grasp, tilting down. Stone cracked, moved, revealing a break in the wall.

The waters rushed into it, pulling the three explorers with them.

And they fell.

Alexandra smacked into a smooth stone surface as she was whisked forward by the waters. Above, the stone wall slid back into place.

They slid down into an unknowable space. Jeffrey and Wallace screamed. Alexandra couldn't find her voice, so only tensed and waited.

Then the stone stopped, replaced by empty air. Alexandra pitched forward, tumbling.

She crashed into water, Jeffrey and Wallace close behind her. With no light, she couldn't sense her up from her down. She clawed at the water, trying to find the surface.

Panic gripped her every muscle. Somehow, courage broke through.

She stopped grasping. She forced her body to settle, to spread out, to float. And she rose, breaching the surface at last. She righted herself and gasped for air.

Behind her, she heard Jeffrey and Wallace floundering, so she swam, grasping at one body and pulling it right. Then the other. The three of them sucked in air and clung to one another, kicking the water and floating like a raft of three friends.

Drips of water plunked into the pool, the echo bouncing all around. Alexandra slapped at the water, listening. The space was vast and empty.

"Which way?" Alexandra asked.

"I've no idea," Wallace said.

"But you just came back this way, right?" Alexandra said. "When you answered the calling."

"I don't remember," Wallace said.

Alexandra turned in the water. She listened for a breeze, anything to hint at a direction.

"Get the flashlight," she said, then tipped forward, lifting the backpack out of the water, her face submerged. She felt Jeffrey work on the zipper, jostling around, then plucking out the flashlight and zipping the pouch closed. He tapped on her shoulder to let her know he was done. She righted herself and swept water off her face.

The flashlight shot light into the cavern. Sheer, flat, stone walls surrounded the large, empty space. Jeffrey guided the beam along the water, searching for and finding stairs that led to an arched doorway with the sunburst emblem carved into the top.

Jeffrey paddled with one arm while keeping the flashlight above his head, leading the three towards the stairs. He stepped out of the water, helping Alexandra up, then

Wallace. Alexandra approached the archway, then reached for the flashlight. Jeffrey handed it over and she swept the beam around the room, finding only high, smooth walls. Above, the stone slide reached up into the ceiling. She couldn't guess how far they'd traveled. Could be twenty feet, could be two hundred feet. It had all happened too fast.

"How did they build this?" Alexandra asked.

"The town provides," Wallace said.

She glanced at Wallace.

"You couldn't have left this way," Alexandra said.

Wallace dipped his head. "I woke up on the pier, and then I found you."

Alexandra turned back to the archway, shining the light through. Beyond was a slick, natural cave. Glistening stalactites hung from the narrow ceiling. There was no obvious way through.

"Do you remember which way to go from here?" Jeffrey asked, looking over Alexandra's shoulder into the cave.

"Well enough," Wallace said, joining them. "We can put on dry clothes. There won't be any more swimming."

"So it's all easy from here?" Alexandra asked, hopeful.

Wallace shrugged. "Would it help if I lied and said yes?"

On the stone walls, Alexandra found chalk drawings of a face with one eye, of the sun emblem, of ships, then a large, crude sketch of the world. The map's proportions were off and Antarctica was missing. There were smaller emblems scattered on the map: a wolf, an eagle, a bear, three stars in a triangle pattern, a moon which was circled and emphatically crossed out.

"Alexandra," Wallace said while pointing to an opening in the cave. "This way."

Alexandra stepped past Wallace and led them into the walkway which tightened and ended after about a dozen feet.

"It doesn't go through," Alexandra said.

"It does," Wallace said.

Alexandra lifted an eyebrow. "This better not be a human sacrifice thing."

"What do you mean?" Wallace asked.

"She thinks we're a cult," Jeffrey said.

"Oh," Wallace said. "I guess we are, but we're a charming kind of cult. Like the Mormons."

"Not helpful," Jeffrey said.

Alexandra turned back to the opening. "You're sure?"

"I am," Wallace answered.

She took off her backpack, then held it in her hand as she knelt down and crawled forward with Wallace behind her. After a hesitation, Jeffrey followed.

The walls were glazed with moisture; the air was musty and stale. The walls narrowed even more; she had to lower herself further to the ground to push forward.

"You're sure this is the way," Alexandra said, pausing.

"The only way is forward," Wallace answered.

Alexandra continued. She knocked her head into a protruding rock, wincing for a moment, then ducked under it. She nudged her backpack ahead of her, the space tightening and lowering until she was almost on her belly, the flashlight gripped in her right fist as she inched forward. Her heart pounded. She felt the oxygen fading.

She pressed on. The ending neared. The beam found a fork. The left seemed to open up, the right she'd have to crawl through.

"Which way?" Alexandra asked.

"Oh," Wallace said.

"Oh? Oh! You don't remember? Is that what you're telling me?"

"Hold on, let me think."

"Take your time, Wallace," Jeffrey said, trying to help.

"It's probably not right," Alexandra said. "That way is really low. If I go that way, I might not get back out if it turns out to be wrong. The left is way easier."

"Go right," Wallace said. "And brace yourself."

"Wait, what?"

Above The Town Where All Things Are Possible,

two mountains stood, protecting the town with a brotherly affection, only allowing the gentlest of weather to pass between their sturdy shoulders. Within the mountains crackled an old magic, coursing like lifeblood deep into their cores and rooting into the earth where their magic converged.

The humans didn't know of the magic in the mountains or of the ancient pact that bound the magic to this land. But all the townspeople and visitors felt it resonate with them as they sang in harmony with the howls of God's Blowhole. The tourists who had no relation to the town and only visited to smirk at the strange customs couldn't resist the musical pull. Hearts swelled, voices merged, and the land glowed and hummed.

Deep below their feet, Alexandra panicked.

Her shoulders were jammed between the tunnel walls as Wallace crawled closer.

"Keep going," he said, voice steady.

"I can't!"

"Try."

"Back up!" Jeffrey called. "Give her space."

Wallace remained steady. "We go forward or we are lost."

Jeffrey, uncertain of what else to do, crawled after Wallace, determined to pull him out of the tunnel if he had to.

"Just a little further," Wallace said. "We are almost there."

"There's no space left!" Alexandra said.

"There is," Wallace said. "I know where we are."

Alexandra tried to pull back, but felt Wallace right

behind her.

"Just a little further," he urged.

Alexandra took a breath, forcing herself to stay calm. Jeffrey took hold of Wallace's waist, trying to pull him back. Alexandra wiggled her shoulders just enough to get free, then flattened herself against the rough floor of the tunnel. She kicked herself forward, feeling the stone press against her sides and her back, her head tapping against the narrowing tunnel.

She'd gone as far as she could.

Then the earth split and they fell.

Above, the chorus heard the hum from God's Blowhole shift to a lower register. The hum silenced, rose again but at a whisper. It silenced once more and would stay silent for another year.

"The Queen's Tide is over!" Margot called to the crowd and they cheered.

The tourists, not understanding the significance, clapped and smirked at one another. Some of the townspeople fetched porch chairs, others spread out blankets, but most simply sat on the cobblestones of downtown. The Greek, Gerald, and a handful of others brought out trays of food and walked through the crowd, letting everyone with an appetite choose from gyros and kabobs and pastries and fresh fruit.

Instruments emerged, songs were played, and children

danced. The tourists struggled to understand how they fit in all of it, but soon were trading stories as if they'd lived in The Town Where All Things Are Possible their entire lives.

Below, the floor dropped into darkness. A cracking sound erupted and the floor began slowing, then stopped so abruptly that Alexandra was nearly thrown off the edge. She flailed for a grip of the edge of the stone surface, throwing an arm over the edge of the floor and letting her backpack and flashlight fall. She watched them tumble below into a vast, glowing purple light.

Wallace and Jeffrey grappled to right themselves on the narrow path that stretched out into darkness in both directions, held up by something beyond their comprehension.

"Get her, Wallace!" Jeffrey said as Alexandra still struggled to pull herself back up.

Wallace looked at Alexandra, a serene smile on his face. He leaned forward and jumped silently down into the glow.

Jeffrey scrambled to Alexandra, grasping her arm. He pulled her back up onto the path. They hugged tightly, now steady on the stone floor. Alexandra looked down at the glow, listening for anything.

"We can try to make our way back along the path," Jeffrey said. "Maybe there is a way up."

Alexandra glanced down at the glow where Wallace had

fallen. *No, not fallen, leapt.*

Jeffrey grasped her hand. "Come on," he said. "There's got to be a way out."

"There is," Alexandra said, then nodding down at the glow.

Jeffrey followed her eyes. He shook his head.

"Come on," Alexandra said, grinning. "It's The Town Where All Things Are Possible."

He pointed up. "No, the town is that way." He pointed down. "That way, I have no idea."

"So let's find out." Her grip tightened. "Together."

And so they leapt.

And this is why we sing

Beneath The Town Where All Things Are Possible,

Alexandra rose from soft, mossy ground to look up at the vegetation all around her. Giant mushrooms, huge blooms framed by fleshy leaves, tall weeds with bursting blossoms.

And it glowed. All of it glowed. Reds, purples, pinks, yellows, blues—its radiance was almost painful to the eye. She winced as she stood, the welt on her head throbbing. She looked down at her feet where Jeffrey still lay, eyes wide, afraid to move.

"Come on, you sweet, silly man," she said, reaching her hand down to him. He took it timidly and allowed her to pull him up to his feet.

Above them was only darkness, but around them was a forest of bioluminescence. Small, vibrant creatures darted from flower to flower. One remained in place just long enough for Alexandra to make out the features of a yellow and green bumblebee. And there, a hummingbird. And there . . .

"Is that a rabbit?" Jeffrey asked, kneeling down to look under a mess of radiant green stalks. The pink rabbit slowly emerged, its ears back, uncertain. It stood, raising its nose to sniff. Jeffrey lowered to his knees and eased his hand out, palm down. The rabbit took a few steps closer, stood again. Its cold nose touched Jeffrey's fingertip. Its coat burst alive with yellows and purples, its inner ears a light blue. It hopped quickly around them and darted into the forest, light tracing its path as it disappeared.

Jeffrey stood. "I can't believe it."

"You never get used to it," Wallace said, and they turned

to see him climbing down from a willow tree. Through its bark, light could be seen traveling up from its roots, into the trunk, and down to the tips of drooping branches.

"Come on," Wallace said, stepping down carefully around a bed of mushrooms. He pointed to the distance. "We're this way."

"We?" Jeffrey asked.

Wallace smiled. "Did you really think I was down here alone?"

Wallace led them through the vibrant colors of the glowing forest as more creatures emerged, curious about the newcomers. A falcon, two deer, a timid cat with piercing yellow eyes. They came to a stream where koi swam in whimsical circles, their scales shimmering in colors that shifted and pulsed.

Wallace hopped over, so Jeffrey and Alexandra followed.

And then they saw it, a grouping of glowing mushrooms as tall as trees, but with wider stems and caps.

"Up there," Wallace said, pointing to the tallest of the mushrooms looming forty feet into the air. Its massive stem was a spiral of oranges and reds with light coiling upwards from the ground.

"How will we get up there?" Alexandra asked.

Wallace smiled, then took a slow step. A smaller mushroom sprouted from the ground just as his foot rested on it. He stepped over it just as another mushroom grew up to meet his footfall. A living staircase grew and curled around the towering mushroom. Wallace climbed as Alexandra and Jeffrey followed.

The mushrooms were sturdier than Alexandra expected.

She kept a hand on the thick stem of the central mushroom to keep her balance. The flesh of the stem was pillowy with hairs that seemed to caress their skin.

"This is the most beautiful and oddly not terrifying thing I've ever seen," Alexandra said.

Wallace smiled back down at her, but said nothing.

"I'm a little terrified," Jeffrey said.

They crested the staircase to find a bed of golden leaves. A thin woman slept underneath them, her back to them. Notecards littered the top of the mushroom cap. Sitting amongst them was Tabitha, looking as if she hadn't aged a day since Alexandra watched her walk away from the dock on her grandfather's land.

"Oh," said Alexandra.

"Oh, indeed," Tabitha said, standing. She crossed over the soft mushroom cap and hugged Alexandra, who remained stiff while looking back at Jeffrey, uncertain how to react.

Tabitha pulled away and took in her very uncomfortable niece. "I get it. A lot to take in."

"So, either we're dead or you're alive," Alexandra said.

Tabitha laughed. "Well, you're definitely alive. I'm somewhere in-between."

"That's some dumb mystical nonsense, auntie," Alexandra said. "Say it like I'm a child."

Tabitha gave Alexandra a playful, stern frown. "That's exactly how I would say it to you if you were a child."

"Fine, fair," Alexandra said. "But I still have no idea what you're talking about."

"She was sick," Wallace said. "The council sent her to me so she could live a bit longer."

"And so I could keep him company," Tabitha added. "For as long as I can manage."

Alexandra glanced down at the young woman beneath the covers. "And she's sick, too?"

"No," Tabitha said. "Just sleeping. She's been asleep for a very long time. Let's see if we can wake her for a bit."

Tabitha crossed over the mushroom cap and knelt down to the woman. Tabitha gently nudged her shoulder, then whispered "Wallace is back. He brought Jeffrey and Alexandra. Would you like to meet them?"

The woman stirred. "They came," she said in a soft, sweet voice. She yawned, then pushed up on her elbow. "I hoped they would."

She turned to face them. Her right eye was a dazzling purple, her left a vibrant green—like two suns burning at different temperatures. "But you never know what to expect with humans."

Beneath The Town Where All Things Are Possible,

a young goddess slept for over two thousand years after a pact was made between gods and animals. It was regarding the troublesome rise of humanity.

"There are just so many of you," the goddess explained to Alexandra, patting a space on the mushroom cap beside her. "That's the problem. That's always been the problem."

Wallace gestured for Alexandra and Jeffrey to join her.

"You're real," Alexandra said, even as she realized the question didn't even approach what she was actually trying to ask. "My ghost in the theatre."

"Yes." The goddess giggled, then yawned wide and loud. "Sorry. It's hard being awake, especially today with so many humans in town. You suck up all the spirit energy, you greedy little creatures."

The goddess sat a little straighter. "I hope I didn't frighten you, but I miss the plays. I miss the gathering of all my family. My lovely little town."

"What do you mean that there are so many of us?" Alexandra asked.

"Each human has a little bit of divinity," the goddess said, then placed a finger against Alexandra's forehead. "Right here. Every one of you. And this was fine for hundreds of thousands of years, but you kept growing and spreading."

The goddess yawned again, then shivered and smiled. "I loved your ways, though. I loved your hope and your vulnerability. So I created a sanctuary for you. Far from the others."

"Humans?" Jeffrey asked

"Gods," Wallace answered.

The goddess smiled sadly. "My sanctuary was not well-received by the others."

"How many gods are there?" Jeffrey asked.

"So many, and they are all asleep because of you." She leaned toward Jeffrey and placed her finger on his forehead. "Because of what you carry here."

She held out her hand to Alexandra. "Do you want to understand?" She held out her other hand to Jeffrey. She looked at both in turn, raised an eyebrow.

They took her hands and their worlds went white. Alexandra gasped, her brain spinning and sinking and melting all at the same time.

She knew the feeling.

The feeling was love.

Then the goddess released them both and they sucked in breaths, nearly tipping backwards. Wallace braced them with a hand on each of their shoulders.

"Steady," the goddess said. "It's a bit much, I know." She yawned again, then watched the couple, curious to hear what they had to say for themselves.

"All of the notes are to you?" Jeffrey asked, regaining himself. "And you grant them their wishes. But then you punish us when the notes don't come?"

"No, she doesn't punish you," Wallace said. "Fate wants balance. The ceremony grants her the power to protect the town, to disrupt fate's balance."

"Like prayers?" Alexandra asked.

"It's how you feed me," she said. "And in return, I give you the tiny miracles that protect you from the cruelty of the world outside. The injustice, the hatred, the brutality."

"But the town has to stay small," Tabitha said. "That's why you don't see luxury hotels, shopping malls, and high rises. We have to keep the town small, or we lose it."

"So if a wish is too big for the town?" Alexandra asked.

Wallace sat down with them, the mushroom bouncing slightly under his weight. "We don't cast anyone out, but the town will let them go seek their miracle out in the world."

"I miss them all," the goddess said. "I call them home every year, not to make them stay, but so that they know that this will always be their home."

The goddess looked at Jeffrey's pocket.

"You brought me a notecard," she asked.

"No," Jeffrey said, covering his pocket. "This one isn't real."

"Then why did you bring it? I already know what it says, you know."

"But," Jeffrey began, but wasn't certain what he wanted to say. He retrieved the note and handed it to her. "It's not real."

She unfolded the notecard. She grinned as she read. Her eyes moved from the card to him.

"Never for me," she said as she held the notecard to her chest. "Never for you. But always and only for us."

"Right," Jeffrey said.

The goddess looked at Alexandra. "Have you read it?"

Alexandra shook her head, unsure of the moment. The goddess handed the note to Alexandra, who unfolded it and read:

I want to leave with Alexandra, whenever and wherever she might go. —Jeffrey

Alexandra felt her heart stir and stretch. The moment was complex, swirling with sadness and love.

"She always wanted to travel," Tabitha said, smiling proudly down at her niece. "She could go find them."

Alexandra looked at her aunt. "Who?"

The goddess sighed. "My idiot brothers."

She closed her green eye, then narrowed her purple eye as she studied Alexandra. The purple iris brightened and glimmered. "Are you up for an adventure, Alexandra?"

Alexandra felt a little hope flutter in her chest. "Always, but—"

The goddess clapped her hands and said "Fabulous. Wendy will know where to guide you."

The goddess started to rise to her feet, but faltered and eased herself back down, dropping the notecard, which tumbled towards the edge of the mushroom cap. Wallace snatched it just before it fell.

Tabitha lowered herself to support the goddess and ease her back down onto the mushroom cap. Tabitha pulled the golden leaves back over her.

"You need to sleep," Tabitha said. She then held out her hand, gesturing for the notecard. Wallace handed it to Jeffrey, who hesitated. Tabitha snapped at him, so Jeffrey handed it over. Tabitha gave it to the goddess, who held it to her chest, cradling it as she settled.

"My brothers are annoying and slow, but they mean

well," the goddess whispered as sleep approached. "The mountains miss them. Agree to find my brothers, and I will release The Man Who Holds The Town Together."

Alexandra smiled and looked at Jeffrey, who was stunned and a little fearful.

"Who will serve the town?" Jeffrey asked, his voice urgent.

"Anyone," the goddess said. "Everyone. Never for me. Never for you. Always and only for us."

Then the goddess slept, leaving the humans to wonder what should come next.

Beneath The Town Where All Things Are Possible,

Alexandra descended the mushroom stairs back to the glowing forest floor. The others followed, including her long lost aunt. At the bottom, Alexandra turned to Tabitha.

"Why didn't you ever reach out to me?" Alexandra asked.

Tabitha sighed, weighing her answer. "I had to respect your parents' wishes. I wanted to, of course. I saw so much of myself in you."

"But even after I was an adult? After my sister died? All this time I told myself it was because you were out battling poachers and sailing from port to port. I thought it was because you never had the time, you were never in one place long enough, but you've been sitting in a quiet bookshop for years."

Tabitha shook her head, her eyes drifting away. "You're right. I should've." She chuckled. "But I thought you'd be out on the high seas too, battling pirates and making your mark."

"I wasn't," Alexandra said. "I should've been."

Tabitha stepped to her niece, squeezed her shoulder. "Then do it now and take him with you."

"We need to get going," Wallace said. "The tide is returning."

They followed Wallace through the forest. He plucked a vibrant purple plum and tossed it back to Jeffrey. He bit into its flesh and his cheeks glowed as he chewed. He swallowed and the glow slid down his throat, disappearing beneath his shirt.

"Wow," Jeffrey said, handing the plum to Alexandra. She

bit into it, a bit of juice dripping down her chin, which he cleared with his finger. She grasped his hand, kissing his finger.

Tabitha watched, smiling.

They continued as owls, foxes, and other uncanny forest life watched. Tabitha fell in with Alexandra and Jeffrey.

"I'm sorry," Tabitha said. "No qualifications, no excuses. I should've written."

Alexandra nodded, taking Tabitha's hand. "It's good to see you again."

And the group walked deeper and deeper into the forest. Above was a starless sky.

"Why did you stop traveling?" Alexandra asked Tabitha. "Once you found the town?"

"The town needed me," Tabitha said. "And I was tired. I was sick, but didn't know it yet." Tabitha reached to her shirt collar, tugging it aside just enough to expose a webwork of bright red veins glowing angry beneath her skin.

Alexandra placed her hand to her mouth, shocked.

"It's okay," Tabitha said. "I had a good run, and I should live at least another year down here. You can come visit next Queen's Tide."

"I'll write to you in the meantime," Alexandra said. "I'll drop it down with the notecards."

"I can't write back," Tabitha said. "It'll only go one way."

"Just knowing you are there to read them, that'll be enough."

They continued walking, approaching a hazy darkness emerging through the lush vegetation. Soon, they reached the edge of the forest. Beyond was only darkness. Tabitha hugged Alexandra, long and tight. Tabitha reached for Jeffrey, pulling him into the hug.

"Thank you," Tabitha whispered to them both. "Now go home."

She pulled away, her hand lingering within Alexandra's as she retreated back into the forest. They turned to Wallace, who stood just before the hazy glow.

"We're running out of time," Wallace said, then stepped into the darkness and disappeared.

Jeffrey laced his fingers around Alexandra's. Together they walked after Wallace.

"Follow my voice," Wallace called, his voice echoing.

The forest floor was gone, replaced by a flat, stone surface. There was no light, only the sound of their footsteps sending echoes against hard, flat walls.

Then another sound. Water moving. Quickly.

"The tide's building!" Wallace said. "Run!"

And they ran blindly forward, following Wallace's echoing steps. The roaring waters neared, and Alexandra sensed they were coming to the end of the space.

"Here, we're here," Wallace said. His hand gripped Alexandra's arm. "This way."

Then came the sound of iron scraping, turning. Light poured in as a heavy door swung open. Beyond was angry, churning water racing through a tunnel.

"Hurry," Wallace said, stepping out onto a steel walkway hanging over the water below. The waters rushed through a dark tunnel towards sunlight beaming down from somewhere in the distance.

"Jump!" Wallace said as he opened a gate that swung just

over the rushing water.

"Into that?" Alexandra asked.

"It's the only way," Wallace said. "And if you don't jump now, the waters will get too high and we'll have to go back and you'll be trapped down here with me."

Jeffrey took Alexandra's hand. "It's okay. I know what this is." Jeffrey grinned back at Wallace. "I've always wanted to do this."

Jeffrey stepped to the edge of the platform, ready to jump down. "Wait," he said, looking over at Alexandra. "You know how to swim, right?"

"What kind of sailor would I be if I didn't?" Alexandra said.

So they leapt. The waters took them immediately, sweeping them off towards the sunlight. Wallace hurried back through the heavy door, closing it just as the waters topped the walkway.

The irresistible force of the water pulled and spun Alexandra and Jeffrey as they struggled to keep their faces above water. There was no swimming, there was only desperate flailing and hope.

They swept hundreds of feet in moments and neared the sunlight where the tunnel ended. Inside a smooth stone chamber, the waters swirled. Within minutes, the tunnel they'd passed through was submerged, but more water rushed in. Alexandra looked up and saw the sunlight beaming through a small opening.

"Where are we?" Alexandra asked, breathless as she kicked to keep above the churning waters.

"Stay—" Jeffrey attempted, but went under. He emerged again, spitting out water. "Stay in the center."

She looked up again, they were approaching the light quickly as the waters flooded the space. The ceiling was criss-crossed with steel girders holding up stone. In the center was the opening and sky far above. She paddled against the whirlpool, reaching the center to join the floundering Jeffrey. She latched onto him. The ceiling was close. They were shooting up, accelerating.

"Watch your head!" Jeffrey shouted.

And they were out, blasted up out of the opening as water surged around them. They tumbled out of the water.

Hands grasped them as they fell, then were lowered softly onto cobblestone. A chorus of cheers followed. Alexandra wiped saltwater from her face and tried to take in the world around her. Nearby, the water still shot up like a geyser.

"God's Blowhole," she said. Around her were all of the townspeople and the astonished tourists. Everyone cheered and danced. Hands patted her on the back. Tessa emerged, checking Alexandra's pupils, feeling her pulse. She smiled and pulled Alexandra to her feet.

Jeffrey was laughing and hugging Leo as they watched the geyser. He hurried to Alexandra and lifted her from the ground and spun her around. He sat her back on her feet and they kissed with sweet, frenzied adrenaline.

The water poured down on dancing children as musicians played. Wendy, the mayor, and Mrs. Gratherson joined

Jeffrey and Alexandra. The mayor held out her hand.

"Welcome to the council," she said.

Alexandra shook her hand, then laughed. "If that's what I had to do to be on the council, what did you have to do to be mayor?"

Margot smiled. "Perhaps one day, you'll find out."

Then they were all swept up into the town's celebration of the end of the Queen's Tide, and many poured into The Tavern Where All Things Are Possible, where Alexandra gratefully accepted a frothy beer from Leo.

"You have to tell me everything," he said, then chucked Jeffrey on the shoulder. "'Cause this sap won't."

As Alexandra settled, a tourist tapped her on the shoulder.

"How did that work?" the tourist asked. "The thing with the geyser."

"God's Blowhole," Alexandra said. "But if I tell you, then there's no mystery, and the mystery is the fun part."

The tourist *tsked* and gave Alexandra a playful, disapproving side eye. "It's like the whole town is in a cult."

"Yup," Alexandra said. "But we're a charming kind of cult."

In The Town Where All Things Are Possible,

the council met beneath the library in the modest boardroom with a rounded table. It smelled musty to Alexandra, but she wasn't sure if it was the time to suggest it being tested for mold. Jeffrey stood before the council, explaining the goddess's proposal.

"There's always been a Man Who Holds The Town Together," Jonathan told his son. "How do we just abandon that after so many generations? After everything my family has sacrificed?"

"Maybe the point is you've sacrificed enough," Mrs. Gratherson said. "I'm for it."

"And my job won't really be done," Jeffrey said. "I'll still manage the notecards and ensure they are in a good place before I leave, and I'll make sure my replacement will know how to keep everything moving while I'm gone. There will still always be a Man Who Holds The Town Together. But it won't always be me."

"Or a man, for that matter," Wendy said. "I've always hated that title."

"And where is it you're going?" Jonathan asked. "And how long will you be gone?"

"We've got breadcrumbs," Wendy said, standing and walking towards the framed sun emblem. She took the painting down, revealing a safe beneath.

"You said you didn't know where they were, you liar," Alexandra snapped, playfully. "And you hid them in the most obvious place in town, behind a stupid painting in the boardroom?"

"You didn't find them," Wendy said, winking.

Alexandra groaned. "I was hoping for adventure."

Wendy unlocked the safe and pulled out five scrolls. "There will be plenty of adventure where you're going." Wendy looked through the scrolls, one at a time, then handing two over to Alexandra, putting the other three back and locking them up for safekeeping.

"And what were those?" Alexandra asked, gesturing to the safe.

Wendy lifted a clever eyebrow. "You're not ready for those. Yet."

In The Town Where All Things Are Possible,

Leo held a notecard between his palms and tried to remember the words.

"Never for me," he began slowly. "Never for you. Always and only for us."

He nodded, looked over to Mrs. Gratherson, who gave him a thumbs up. He knelt down and slipped the notecard through the storm grate. Dozens of townspeople surrounding him cheered. Leo stood up awkwardly. He patted his legs, looking around with an awkward smile.

"Is that really it?" he asked, receiving hearty pats on the back. "Wasn't so bad at all."

As the town dispersed into the night towards their homes, Gerald and Tessa stole back to God's Blowhole and slipped an envelope bearing "To Tabitha, Wallace, and our new friend," written in Alexandra's handwriting. It fluttered down God's Blowhole.

Right into Wallace's waiting hands.

Far From The Town Where All Things Are Possible,

Alexandra and Jeffrey lay beneath a blanket on the deck of a catamaran and gazed up at the night stars. Beside her were the two scrolls that would guide them on their search for the goddess's idiot brothers. Jeffrey was drifting to sleep as Alexandra thought of the small rowboat she'd absconded with as a child. Her and her sister. She'd lost her oars, and that was her mistake. One she'd never make again.

And perhaps when they found these gods, they would make her another bargain, one that would lead her back to her sister. She would save her this time, because the world was new to Alexandra. And in this world, anything was possible.

THE END

Author's Note

I originally wrote this novel as a weekly writing challenge where I'd write and post a chapter of a novel once a week on social media. This followed a two year daily writing challenge where I'd create a flash fiction story inspired on Dicitonary.com's word of the day.

This manic pace was an effort to loosen up my writing and force me to create on demand without waiting for inspiration to reveal itself.

I distinctly remember when the first version of the story took a wrong turn. It was years ago when Literati Press was still just a tiny publishing company based out of my bedroom. We'd just had a successful release of a comic series named *Heathen*, giving us a glimmer of optimism we might be ceating something really special in Oklahoma City. I'd been so starved for community as a younger writer that I hoped that Literati Press might grow to become the very thing I'd spent decades looking for. We could and should create it so that the next generation of writers might have an easier path.

With that optimism in mind, I began writing *In The Town Where All Things Are Possible*.

I was surprised at how easily the story flowed and how nice it felt to create something hopeful and sweet-natured. Yet as a weekly deadline loomed halfway through the novel, I panicked that it all seemed too hopeful and too sweet-natured. Without some grim conflict underneath it all, who would buy into the idea of this little town?

So I took the coward's way out and invented conflict to

carry the book to the end.

I've always regretted it, so as the fifteenth year anniversary approachd for Literati Press, I realized the question was no longer "Can we build a community where all things are possible," but rather "How can we keep this community we've already built alive for generations to come?"

You see, we'd opened a bookshop since this book's first draft. We'd also started a Writers Co-Op. We'd also published titles that had reached every corner of the world. We'd also created a performance space for ambitious storytellers to bring brave original works.

We'd built our little town. So I decided to rewrite this novel to reflect not what I believed might be possible, but what I *knew* was possible.

This book is for all the writers, editors, illustrators, designers, readers, advocates, and book concierges who've helped keep Literati Press a force for change in Oklahoma City's literary community.

And also to my wife and the rest of my family and friends who've stuck with me despite all the sacrifices and setbacks we've encountered along the way.

And finally to any aspiring writers who've yet to find their community. I promise that your people are out there, just waiting to be found.

Charles J. Martin
Literati Press Bookshop & Community
Summer, 2025

The Martin & Weinke Continuum

From the escapades of a rock sprophet to the global culling of humanity by Mother Nature, the Martin & Weinke Continuum connects standalone novels tracing our stumbling march to the end of civilization and beyond. These satirical, character-focused, and cross-genre stories examine our tenuous perch atop the food chain and what happens when everything else on the planet, both natural and unnatural, decides it's time for humans to be dethroned.

In order of continuity:

- *the dominant hand*
- *Deviants*
- *How To Control Gravity and Other Stories*
- *In The Town Where All Things Are Possible*
- *Pets*
- *Edward & The Island*
- *Edward & The Wilderness*
- *Edward & The Infinite*